SNOW ANGELS

and other short stories

Harriet Loveday

Harriet Loveday Romance

Thank you, Theresa and Gill, for your continued support. Thank you, Numbers - for allowing me to believe again.

CONTENTS

PREFACE

I have a few favourite Christmas stories. I remember particularly *The Little Match Girl*. My parents didn't have much money when I was growing up, so at primary school I was rarely allowed a book from the book catalogues the school sent home. Except. One Christmas my mum ordered *The Little Match Girl* for me. Not only was the book special because I was almost never allowed books from the catalogue; it had beautiful artwork (I can still see the pictures in my mind of a little girl huddling up against a match); but because I could empathise with the little girl, and it all seemed so unfair. I was also blessed to have a granny that loved me, just like the little girl. I know we are watched over by those that love us – don't you just feel the same in your heart?

Snow Angels, the title story, is a modern take on *The Little Match Girl*. Hopefully it will remind us that ultimately, we are loved, be it in this world or the next. And that someone is always watching over us.

Happy Christmas.

HL x (December 2022)

1. LOVE AS SOFT AS SNOWFLAKES

'Hello?' Walter said in his nicest voice, as he craned his head over the garden fence, to catch another glimpse of her in the fading, twinkling, evening light.

'Hello?' he tried again.

My goodness she was beautiful. Skin as white as snow, her eyes were coal black, and over her straw-coloured, golden hair she had the sweetest, little, pink, fluffy, bobble hat. Cute as a button.

Walter attempted to straighten his own tatty hat (that he was wearing to keep off the snow) and smiled his best smile. She turned to face him, and dropping her eyes to the snow at her feet, gave him the sweetest smile.

Walter's heart fluttered. He knew. He just knew. She was the one. After all these years, here she was. As if she was created just for him. His soul mate.

Walter tried to engage her in conversation again. 'It's chilly, isn't it? Although I see you have your hat.' He nodded towards the house as he continued in a gentle, conversational tone. 'You must be new here? Just moved in?'

Again, she dropped her eyes and smiled. Then, oh

how his heart skipped a beat, she gently raised her eyes to his and said, 'Yes, just yesterday.'

Their eyes locked and little snowflakes danced around them happily, as the moment stretched and stretched a little longer. Walter's heart did back-flips and he tried to do everything he could not to mess up. Steadily he held her gaze and across all time and all worlds, they secured their connection. They had finally found each other.

Walter forged on bravely, secure in the knowledge that she was the one. 'You know, I hope you don't mind me saying, but, well, you have a lovely smile.' She blushed and dropped her eyes before raising her eyes to his again. He continued, 'Please, tell me, what is your name?'

'Crystal. It's Crystal . . . What's yours?' she softly replied. Her voice was as light as the breeze.

'Walter. It's a family name I believe. Not that I've met any of the Walters that have gone before me.' He shook his head, trying to bury the thought that he felt so very alone. He didn't want her to know. He didn't want to scare her away.

Walter looked up. Crystal didn't seem scared or afraid of him. She hadn't moved from where she stood in the back garden. She just continued to look at him gently. He really felt as if he could speak to her about anything. Any subject. He didn't feel judged. He felt warm and safe. He felt like he'd found home.

Crystal said, kindly, 'It's always been one of my favourite names.'

Walter tried not to blush at the compliment. Smiling, he looked slightly away and desperately tried to think of something cheerful to say on this cold, clear evening.

'I love the decorations.' Walter said. 'The icicle lights look so pretty against the dark blues of the sky. It really makes you feel so Christmassy, doesn't it?' Walter looked from the white, hanging, icicle lights adorning her house, back to Crystal.

'Do you know?' Crystal said, opening up, 'Christmas is just my favourite time of the year. I love it. The warmth and generosity. The fun and the laughter. Everything decorated and adorned. It really seems so very special, magical almost. It's the only time of year that I really feel *alive*.'

Walter felt very grateful, that this beautiful woman had shared something so personal with him. It made him feel special, as if she was telling him her secrets, because she trusted him. His eyes were slightly moist as he replied, 'From now on, Crystal, this will be my favourite time of year too.'

In comfort and security, their eyes held on to each other, as if they were the only two people in the world. The cold, snowy gardens; the shimmering evening air; the houses; the smoking chimneys; the chatter and the dogs from somewhere inside – it was as if all these things were a blur, nothing more than a spiral of white noise around them. Whereas inside the swirling world, quite still, quite calm, stood Crystal and Walter, as if they had always been and would forever be.

3

Walter smiled at Crystal, and Crystal smiled at Walter. He felt more and more comfortable to talk to her, ask her questions and get to know her. So, they chatted quietly together until it was too late, too dark and too cold. Walter promised her, and he meant it, that they would talk again soon, before they wished each other goodnight.

* * *

It was the very next evening that Walter saw Crystal again. He had missed her. The time without her had been cold and lonely. His heart had longed for her beautiful dark eyes resting gently in his. The time had passed so slowly, it had been agony, but now, as he craned his head over the fence again to check, he could see . . . there she was!

Crystal was wearing the same cute, little, pink, fluffy hat. Walter's heart melted instantly. The time without her had felt like a cold eternity, now that she was here, all he wanted was to bask in her presence, to stand beside her and feel home. As long as he could be with her and feel her magic, then that would be enough. Life could keep all its excitements and adventures. He knew with certainty that she was all he ever wanted.

'Crystal?' Walter gently called to her. 'Crystal? It's Walter. From next door. How are you?'

Crystal turned to him and their eyes connected. She was here and he was complete. His heart let out a deeply held sigh of fear, which evaporated into the icy evening air.

'Walter? I'm so happy to see you.' Crystal said, blushing and looking at her feet as if she had said too much.

'I hope I didn't talk too much yesterday? I hope you weren't cold? Do tell me if you get too cold.' Walter said with concern in his voice.

'Not at all. I'm quite cosy.' From under her thick eyelashes, her dark eyes peaked up at the hat on her head. Looking back at him she smiled as she said, 'It was lovely talking to you yesterday.'

Walter's heart soared. He wanted to hold on to this moment and make it last forever. He thanked the gods and the wind; he thanked the angels and the elves. Whoever had delivered this wonderful woman to him clearly had a heart.

Trying to capture his soaring heart and place it back inside his body, Walter gulped, smiled, and said, 'So, do you have any plans for Christmas this year? Family? Friends?'

Sadly, Crystal shook her head, 'No, it's just me this year. And the cat.'

Walter had seen the cat earlier, chasing the birds from his bird table. Little rascal. Walter smiled widely. 'Could I be so bold, I mean, that is to say, please don't feel any pressure, but perhaps you'd like to lunch with me over Christmas? I'm not a great cook, but it would be my pleasure to cook for you.'

The invitation hung heavily in the air.

Crystal replied, 'I would love that, that would

be wonderful,' Crystal stumbled over her words slightly, 'I mean, thank you. Yes.'

'Is there anything you don't like to eat? Just so I can be prepared.' Walter asked.

'Carrots. I'm not very fond of carrots. Other than that, my tastes are pretty simple.' Crystal replied.

They smiled at each other over the garden fence.

Now that Walter had secured a future date with her, he relaxed a little bit. As long as he didn't say something daft, he would definitely be seeing her again for Christmas lunch. Walter felt emboldened to ask some of the questions he hadn't been brave enough to ask yesterday.

'So, you're single? A beautiful woman like you shouldn't be alone.'

Crystal shrugged. 'I just, I've never found the right guy.' The smile fell slightly from her face.

Walter promptly said, 'I'm so sorry, I don't want to upset you.'

Quickly, Crystal replied, 'No, not at all.' She took a deep breath and continued, 'I don't want to be with someone that isn't right for me. I don't want arguments, or upset, or someone that treats me as a trophy. I'd rather be alone than with someone that doesn't care.' Crystal sighed deeply, letting out a long-held hurt. 'So, I've been alone.' she said.

Walter looked pained. She was hurting. She'd been lonely. He wanted to leap over the fence and hold her, kiss her forehead and tell her not to worry. He wanted to tell her that she'd never feel alone again. His heart was in twisted agony that she was hurting, and in that moment, he would have moved the world to protect her from this pain.

Crystal continued, 'But,' and she looked at him, smiling gently, 'I just have a good feeling in my tummy that I don't need to worry anymore. That waiting for the right person to come into my life was the right thing to do.'

It was him! She was referring to him! She was telling him that she had waited all this time and that everything he was feeling about her was reciprocated, that she felt the same way about him as he did about her.

With a tiny tear in his eye, Walter said, 'You never need to feel lonely again. Just let me know. I will be there.' Smiling he added, 'Oh and my hugs are free! Anytime. It's no bother.'

The cat wound around Crystals feet as she replied, 'Thank you, Walter. I would like that.' Crystal gave him one of her soft, gentle smiles.

Walter tried to stem the rivers of emotional love that were washing over his body. Desperately he looked around the garden for a subject to discuss and to lighten the tone. Brightly, he said, 'I see you are a keen gardener; you have cut down a lot of the trees. Do you have plans for the garden?'

Crystal looked around her garden and replied, 'I like the light. I like the sunshine full on my face. It warms me somehow. I haven't really thought what to do about the garden yet. I don't really know much about gardening, but I'm sure I'll learn, come the spring. And you, do you have any plans?'

Walter similarly looked around his dark, over-grown garden, with tall trees and shrubs that should have been trimmed *years* ago. It really was a mess, what must she think of him? Clearing his throat, he grandly said, 'I'm fond of water features. I'd like a fountain. This year I was thinking of really getting on and doing something about the garden.' Quietly he added, 'I know it's a bit of a mess.'

'Not at all.' Crystal defended him, 'We all have so little time. The most important thing is to use the time you have wisely. You can't get it back, can you? I'd rather live and feel in the moment, than do chores for eternity.'

Walter looked relieved and they smiled at each other over the fence. Just as the evening before, they chatted together late into the night. Not once did Crystal complain of the cold. Their hearts were quite warm.

※ ※ ※

The next day was bright and sunny, and mild. Walter's overgrown garden didn't see much of the warm winter sun, and so the snow persisted. But Crystal's garden was in the full force of the sun's sparkling rays, and the snow became quite slushy. Even the cat decided the ground was too sludgy to hunt on and spent most of the day lying in front of the full-length, glass, back door, watching the garden.

Almost as if it was an engagement, something that was pre-determined; when dusk started to fall, and the evening stars came out to twinkle their light, Walter came out in the garden and hopefully craned his head over the fence.

Crystal wasn't there.

Perhaps he was early? Looking up at the sky he could see a shooting star. He tried to remember what he'd been told about shooting stars. Not quite remembering he decided it was lucky, because he felt lucky. All day he had pined for her, waiting for this moment to be near to her, and bask in her presence.

Walter waited and waited. But still Crystal didn't come.

Walter watched the cat leave the house and jump his fence. He watched it eye the bird table. He heard it torment some small animals in the hedge behind him, and after having its fun, it walked back across his garden, eyeing him warily. "Little monkey." he thought to himself. But he was trying to distract his increasingly panicking heart. Where was Crystal? Surely, she'd be here soon?

Walter tried to console himself. Thank goodness he'd asked her about spending Christmas with him. At least he knew he'd see her again. No carrots. He mustn't forget or mess up. No carrots.

Trying not to look like a mad man, Walter bravely craned his head over the fence again. Where was she? From somewhere far away, carried on the cold winter breeze in a clear December sky, Walter heard a church clock chime twelve. Had he really been here that long? His heart sank with disappointment.

All Walter wanted was to feel her presence and share her smile, to look into her eyes and connect with her. She was all he wanted. It was physically painful, waiting and hoping she might come out. Without a care for the time or the cold, Walter stood there, waiting.

The morning hours chimed themselves in. Each one was like an ice-shard to his ever-freezing heart. Every part of him hoped to see her. Where was his Crystal? He knew she was his, just as he would be forever hers.

The dawn light started to lift the horizon. Bravely, Walter shuffled over to the garden fence and looked fully in, just as the sun was starting to rise.

There, on the ground, where Crystal had stood the evenings before, lay a discarded pink, fluffy hat, some straw, two coals and a carrot, in a muddy puddle.

Crystal?

The sun lifted its heavy weight above the horizon and shone full-strength into the garden. Walter's eyes dripped little tears in the bright light.

Crystal?

Staring at the muddy puddle where his love had once stood, Walter's heart started to melt and his tatty, old hat slid off his head.

Somewhere in the universe the sands of time flipped over. Walter and Crystal's time had come to an end.

2. A GIFT OF BEAUTY

Miss Collingate sat back heavily in her near thread-bare chair and lifted her tired legs up onto the pouffe. The little bungalow had been her late mother's and she hadn't really had much of a care to redecorate since her mother had passed away. Besides, it was only her and the dogs.

The fire in the grate in front of her glowed warmly, and beside her she had a little hot toddy to see herself to bed. In tiredness and weariness, she ran her hand back over her forehead to where a tight bun held back her black, now greying hair. She could feel the wrinkles of stress and time over her face, but she tried not to think of it, and closed the world out from her big brown eyes.

Lucy Collingate had spent the day in the garden, digging up the last of the winter potatoes. Her hands were tough, chapped and dirty. No matter how hard she scrubbed her hands, the dirt clung to her nails. Absentmindedly she picked up a pile of schoolbooks, ready to do a little marking before bed. She'd decided to switch on the TV to keep her company, when her two black labradors jumped up and started barking loudly.

'Now Blitzen, now Dancer. Enough.' But the dogs

weren't ready to sit back quietly. They needed to let her know. Someone was here.

Lucy was the last bungalow at the end of a lane, a few miles out of town. There were a few streetlights, but they didn't reach as far as her little house. Unless someone had a need, no one came down here, particularly at this time of night, in winter. Unless it was those troublesome school kids again. How did they get her address? Screaming cruel jibes at her from behind the hedge. Jibes that in her saddest soul she believed to be true. She was a spinster and she was alone. Lucy decided she would talk to the headmaster about it tomorrow.

The dogs stood proud in her living room and barked again.

Woof, woof, woof. Woof, woof, woof.

Lucy sighed and put the schoolbook she was about to mark back on the pile. Eagerly the dogs ran to the front door, desperate to dash outside and hunt out the visitor.

Lucy pulled back the curtains and looked out of the large front window in her living room. All was quiet and dark outside. She could make out the wide gravel drive and the trees lining the little lane beyond. Further on in the distance she could see the town of St. Austell on the other side of the valley. Its orange and white glare was a little beacon of civilization in this dark, damp, cold night.

Blitzen and Dancer rushed back to Lucy and stood to attention beside her, sniffing at the glass and straining their eyes. Every part of their bodies

13

were straight and taught. Ready for action.

Lucy knew she would have no peace until she let them sniff out the poor cat or fox that had happened to cross their territory. So, followed by two bouncing, eager dogs, she went through to the hall, pulled on her winter coat and boots, grabbed a flashlight, and unlocked the front door.

The dogs were off like whippets out of the starting cage.

Still standing in the doorway, Lucy flicked on the outside lights for the drive, just in time to see their black bodies disappear out of the wide-open front gates and off up the lane. Sighing again, and lamenting the loss of her warm fire, Lucy diligently closed the door, switched on her flashlight, and crunched over the drive after them.

As Lucy reached the end of her drive, she found the dogs hadn't gone very far. She could hear them not more than fifty metres away.

Woof, woof, woof. Woof, woof, woof.

In reply to their barks she heard, 'Help! Help! Don't bite me. Somebody, help!' It was an older voice, high for a man, certainly not children.

Jogging a little along the slushy, muddy, damp lane, Lucy rushed to the centre of the commotion. Her torch bobbing before her like a lifeboat on a stormy sea.

Suddenly, there in the flashlight, she saw a pile of old clothes and a big bushy beard of a thin man, pressed back against the hedge. The rucksack he had been carrying was discarded in the lane a little way from him. His hands were defensively trying to block the dogs from attacking him. Although, as any animal lover would know, this wasn't an attack. Blitzen and Dancer were furiously wagging their tails as if their lives depended on it. Blitzen was sniffing the man's clothes and Dancer almost managed to lick the man's hand.

In agony and fear the man cried, 'Dogs! Dogs! Call them off. They're attacking me.'

Lucy pulled up level with the petrified pile of clothes that was a man. Her dogs danced around in delight at the new friend they had found.

'I'm so sorry.' Lucy said kindly, holding the flashlight over the dogs so that he could see their flopping tongues and flapping tails, 'They're just excited to see you. They don't want to hurt you.' And with that Lucy commanded the exuberant animals to sit.

Blitzen and Dancer really did try, but their bottoms kept wiggling and their wagging tails gave the impression that they were propelling themselves across the lane to him, about to pop up again any minute.

The man looked out from behind his raised hands, from where he had partially fallen against the hedge. His faced was lined and thin. Dirt held to the cracks and his skin had almost a grey hue, and seemed damp, not unlike the dark, damp night they found themselves in. His hair had been left to grow and it sprouted from every orifice. His beard appeared to be a browny-colour, but had bursts of red and grey, not unlike an artist's impression. On his head he wore a waxed walking hat, held down tight with a toggle that disappeared under his chin. Around his body were layered various sorts of clothes: at least two jackets and bits of jumper poked out here and there, all in shades of grey, brown and muted khaki; these were tied at his waist by a piece of orange binder's twine. Protruding from the bottom of the rags were two ginger-coloured, corduroy trouser legs, which flapped about some very skinny shins underneath. His feet were protected by some well-worn, Gore-Tex walking boots.

The man looked petrified.

'I'm so sorry.' Lucy said again. 'We didn't mean to scare you. They're just excited to meet you that's all. Here, let me pass you your bag.' So saying, Lucy stooped down and passed the man his rucksack, which had a little sleeping bag securely held underneath. The rucksack was damp from where it had been discarded in the lane, but not too badly. It rattled as she handed it to him. The sound reminded Lucy of the pencil tins the children brought to school.

Carefully the man reached his hands towards her and pulled his rucksack into him, clutching it tightly. 'I don't like dogs.' He managed to say again. He looked warily at the black labradors, bottom shuffling at his feet, and craning forward to try and lick him.

Lucy tried to change the subject. 'Can I help you?

Were you looking for a particular house?' She indicated further up the lane to the gate lights of one of her neighbours.

The man gulped and shook his head, "No."

Lucy tried again. 'Perhaps a cup of tea and a biscuit might help? It is a bit of a cold, damp night.'

As soon as she said the words "tea" and "biscuit" she could see a little glimmer in the man's cold, tired, blue eyes. Involuntarily the man licked his lips. Lucy could tell he was hungry and likely homeless. He was also scared. She felt sorry for him.

'I have just put the kettle on.' (Lucy lied). 'Why don't you come back with me and have a cup of tea and a biscuit for five minutes?'

The man hesitated and looked at the dogs.

Lucy took control. 'Well, the offer is there if you want it. I must get back now. Goodnight.' Whistling to the dogs, she started to walk back down the lane, with the desperate dogs diligently following her heels, and holding their heads low, while sneaking glances back at their goodbye friend.

'Wait!' cried the man. 'Oh wait! That's kind. A cup of tea would be lovely. Please wait.' Lucy stopped and turned around, while the man hobbled up to her. As he drew near, he said, 'Gabriel.' He held out his hand.

Lucy took his large, skinny hand in her chapped, rough one, and they shook. 'Lucy.' Lucy simply replied and smiled. 'Come on then.' She flicked the flashlight towards the entrance of her bungalow.

As she did so she noticed the man's face light with hope and fear. Lucy started walking again and whistled to her dogs to follow her. Gabriel obediently trotted alongside her too.

When they reached the gravel drive and crunched towards the bungalow, Gabriel looked about himself in fear, as if some ghost or ghoul were about to jump out at him from the hedge at any moment. When they reached the step at the front door, and Lucy removed her key, Gabriel looked terrified and stuttered, 'No. No. I won't come in. I'll just sit on the step. Thank you.'

Lucy looked at him with a puzzled brow. Was she really so terrifying? Kindly she said, 'It's cold out here. Do come in for a cup of tea.'

But Gabriel was insistent. 'No. No. I'll just sit here. Thank you.'

Lucy couldn't very well force him in. So, leaving him on the step, she entered the bungalow with her dogs, shut the door against the cold and, after removing her boots and coat, went through to her little kitchen. Within a few minutes she was back at the door, with a large mug of warm, milky tea, a couple of biscuits in wrappers and a large slice of carrot cake.

Gabriel wobbly stood to standing, his eyes were alight at the goodies before him. Thanking Lucy, he immediately took the wrapped biscuits and stowed them in his pocket. Then gratefully receiving the tea and cake, he sat back down in the cold and the damp, to eat his supper.

Lucy asked kindly, 'Do you have anywhere to stay tonight?'

Gabriel eyed Lucy wearily, then deciding she could be trusted, shook his head sadly, "No."

Lucy sighed for him. She knew it was a risk. 'Look, I have my brother's old room. It's not a hotel, but it is out of the cold. Would you like to stay there tonight? Perhaps we could call a homeless shelter tomorrow?'

Gabriel quickly replied, 'No room. No shelter. The shelters are full of drug addicts. I don't want to go there.'

'But you can't stay out in the damp and the cold.'

Gabriel shook his head stubbornly, "No." Then he appeared to have a flash of inspiration. 'Do you have a shed? A garden shed?' he asked. His eyes looked bright. 'Perhaps I could stay in your shed tonight?'

Lucy set her mouth in a grim line. Yes, she did have a shed, but it would likely touch freezing tonight. That was no place to be. But she did have her parent's old touring caravan in the field behind the bungalow. That might work.

'I have my parent's old caravan. I'm not sure of the state of it. But perhaps you'd like to stay there?'

Gabriel's eyes were as wide as saucers, as he repeated her words. 'A *caravan*.' He said finely. As if this were the height of luxury. 'Thank you so very much. I would be very grateful to stay in your caravan for the night.'

The tramp and the teacher smiled at each other.

Finally, they had negotiated their agreement.

✳ ✳ ✳

Leaving Gabriel on the steps, Lucy re-entered the bungalow and commanded her brain to think efficiently. Taking a large shopping bag from under the sink, she quickly filled it with: a thermos of boiling water, a mug into which she stuffed some teabags, a pack of rich tea biscuits, some apples, a pack of wet wipes, some toilet paper (she tried not to think about this, but if he wasn't going to enter the house then the field was his only option), a spare blanket and pillow and a torch.

Lucy had last been in the caravan in the autumn. There were a few spider's webs and it had smelt a little musty, but it also still had gas in the little gas heater, so at least he would be warm. The caravan wasn't connected to the water or electric, otherwise it was okay.

Returning to the hall, Lucy put her coat and boots back on. Her dogs were eagerly twisting around her legs and happily licking their lips. Opening the door, she found Gabriel just where she'd left him. He looked up at her kindly.

Trying not to make eye contact she said, 'I've grabbed a few essentials. This will see you through tonight. The caravan isn't connected to the water or the electric at the moment, but we can look into that. That is, if you want to stay more than one night.' Again, she was careful not to look at him and instead pretended to be busy with the dogs. 'But there is a gas heater,' she continued, 'just don't leave it on overnight when you're asleep.'

Little tears pricked Gabriel's eyes at Lucy's kindness. 'Of course. No, I won't. Thank you, Lucy.' he said.

As he said her name she looked up and met his tender blue eyes with her big brown ones. For all of a few seconds, she felt young and seen again. Not old and tired. Lucy shook the thought away and gave a brief smile, as she placed the empty mug and plate back inside the bungalow, and closing the front door, directed Gabriel around the side of the property, through the field gate, towards the caravan.

Conversationally, Gabriel asked, 'So what is it that you do?'

'I'm a teacher,' Lucy replied. 'Maths. Yourself?' as soon as she said the words, she regretted it. Obviously he was a tramp. He didn't *do* anything.

'I'm an artist.' Gabriel simply replied.

'Oh!'

'Yes, I do portraits mainly. I actually have some of my work in the National Portrait Gallery in London.' Then his voice trailed off sadly. 'But that was a long time ago.'

Lucy tried to remain chipper. 'Well, that's certainly a talent. I think I have some art materials from school in the bungalow if you like? That is, if you still do your art?'

'Do you? Perhaps I could draw you? As a thank

you.' As soon as he'd said it, Gabriel regretted it. Lucy didn't answer and just looked away, busying herself with the caravan door and the flashlight. Gabriel stood patiently behind her, holding the shopping bag.

Showing Gabriel inside, Lucy was able to quickly update him on how to unfold the bed; re-emphasised not to use the toilet; reiterated that the caravan wasn't plugged into the water and electric, but that she could sort it; showed him how to use the gas fire, and reminded him not to leave it on overnight. Shooing the dogs out, she wished him goodnight.

As she turned to leave, Gabriel said, 'Lucy?'

'Yes?'

Gabriel paused slightly, 'Did you know your name means light? Like a light in the darkness?'

'No, I didn't.'

Gabriel fell silent before lifting his head to continue, 'Thank you, Lucy. Goodnight.'

Teacher and artist nodded each other goodnight.

※ ※ ※

It was at least a week before Gabriel felt confident enough to come into the bungalow for a bath. He was even brave enough to let Lucy have a go at cutting his hair with her brother's old clippers. It was almost quite fun to experiment at playing hairdressers. It wasn't as if Lucy could make it any worse.

Gabriel looked rather different after his hair was neatly tidied away, and his beard was no more than a trim around his chin. Gabriel liked to wear it with a thin moustache on top and a little goatee underneath. Lucy wasn't overly sure, but that was what he wanted, so she let him be. Once the dirt was cleaned from his wrinkles, they weren't so noticeable, and with less hair on his head, Gabriel's blue eyes were really quite enchanting. Lucy also dug out some of her brother's old clothing. Gabriel was so skinny that it all fitted with room to spare. Lucy tried not to think of her brother when she saw the same familiar tops, she tried not to think of what he would make of this if he was still alive, instead she was pragmatic and glad they were being put to good use. It was a good thing that she'd never got around to clearing out his clothes and donating them to charity. Perhaps it was fate.

The time raced towards Christmas before Gabriel finally agreed to come into the house for an evening meal. Lucy and Gabriel had settled into a routine where he would come in to bath twice a week, and he would walk the dogs for her while she was at school during the day. She'd even noticed that he'd been brave enough to pet Blitzen and Dancer *and* give them treats. The dogs just adored him.

Lucy and Gabriel had also agreed that for Christmas Day he would come to church with Lucy in the morning, then come into the house for Christmas lunch, and stay to hear the King's speech afterwards, before returning to his caravan.

Lucy hung up a little wooden train adorned with festive glitter on her fake Christmas tree, as she mused that it would be strange spending Christmas in company this year. She was always so used to being alone. She'd thought about getting Gabriel a present to put under the tree, but she knew that he couldn't afford to get her one, and she didn't want to embarrass him, so she buried the thought.

Placing tealights in little candle holders on the mantlepiece, Lucy caught sight of herself in the mirror. Although she was used to looking old, it was always a shock. She didn't know if it was the sadness she'd passed through or the normal ravages of time. Her hair was slick back in a harsh bun. It was mainly black but with ever increasing streaks of grey. Wrinkles were etched over her forehead, around her eyes and her mouth was bracketed by deep lines and jowls. If she didn't smile, she looked decidedly grumpy. Lucy looked away quickly. She didn't think she was grumpy. Just quiet. Just kept to herself. That's all.

✼ ✼ ✼

Lucy found that she was rather looking forward to Christmas Day this year. It felt different. She was going to have company. She wasn't going to be alone. Also, Gabriel was pleasant to be around. He told her interesting things, but he didn't interfere, or intrude, or outlast his welcome.

Gabriel attended church with Lucy in the morning and quietly sang along to the carols. He was comfortable to come for tea, biscuits and mince pies after the service, and Lucy delicately introduced him as her "friend". Everything was polite and easy.

Lucy had prepared most of the lunch the evening before. She had left the turkey and potatoes roasting gently in the oven while they were at church, but what little there was still to do after the service, Gabriel was more than happy to do. Taking the oven gloves from Lucy's tired, thick hands, he said, 'Here. Let me. You sit down. I need to do my share.' and in so doing he kindly finished the last of the cooking and serving up for her.

Lunch was pleasant. The dogs sat around Gabriel's chair, not Lucy's. She was sure she saw him slipping a little of his turkey to them under the table. She tried not to look, or to smile. Particularly considering how scared he'd been of them the first night they'd met. Blitzen and Dancer just adored him and the sentiment appeared to be mutual.

After sitting next to the fire in the living room to listen to the King's speech on TV, and drinking a warming Christmas sherry, Gabriel thanked Lucy and made ready to leave. He hadn't noticed the only present sitting under the Christmas tree.

'Thank you for a lovely Christmas, Lucy.' Gabriel looked down at the floor, as he sat on the edge of his seat, ready to go. Sentimentally he added, 'Everything in my life has improved since you have been here for me. You really are a shining light.

Happy Christmas.'

Lucy found she had a lump in her throat. Trying to swallow and speak, Lucy managed to say, 'I've got you a little something.' Gabriel flushed slightly with embarrassment. He didn't have a present for Lucy. Lucy ploughed on, 'It's just a little thing. I don't want you to be embarrassed.' Standing up and reaching under the tree she brought out a wide flat package with a bump in the middle of it. Without making eye contact she handed it to him.

Gabriel looked embarrassed, but he was gracious and would certainly kindly accept the gift. Running his thin fingers under the wrapper he said, 'Lucy you are so kind. I didn't get you anything.' Lucy shook the thanks and concerns away. She had her dogs, her house and her job. She didn't need presents, she had everything she needed.

Folding back the paper, Gabriel gave a little cry of surprise. 'Oh! How clever of you. This is just right.' Gabriel seemed quite animated and excited, he forgot to be embarrassed as he beamed at Lucy. The dogs craned their heads over his lap, to see what was inside the cheap, bright-red paper.

On Gabriel's lap sat a pad of professional art paper and a tin of art pencils.

Gabriel opened the tin in excitement and looked pleased as he held some of the pencils aloft. 'Oh!' he said happily, 'This is quite the thing. Exactly right. Thank you, Lucy.'

For the first time Lucy really allowed herself to smile. She was happy for him. She was happy that she'd made him happy.

Gabriel sat opposite her captivated. 'Do you know?' he said, really connecting with her eyes for the first time since they'd met, 'You really are so beautiful when you smile.'

Lucy felt her face glow warm in the heat of the fire and looked away quickly.

Gabriel continued, 'You have been so kind to me, a stranger. Never once have you questioned me or said a cross word. You have given me this very thoughtful gift,' Gabriel looked down happily at Lucy's gift on his lap, 'and now, it is my turn to return the favour. Lucy, would you allow me to draw you?' Lucy was about to protest, her mouth forming a horrified "No." but Gabriel managed to say first, 'As my Christmas present to you. It is only fair.'

Lucy didn't want to embarrass him and she didn't want to reject him. So begrudgingly, she hesitated and didn't say, "No."

'Wonderful!' Gabriel continued. 'I think, this will be the best setting, just as you are, in your chair, happy.' Lucy had never really considered herself *happy* before, but she allowed Gabriel the space to continue. 'Only, I think, if you don't mind, would you let down your hair? I think the dark of your hair would frame your face well and make for a better portrait.'

Lucy felt very self-conscious as she complied. But she felt that as this was now his gift, she was duty-bound to allow him this. It was only fair.

Gently, Gabriel arranged Lucy's hair around her shoulders, and lightly touching her face, he tilted it to just the angle he wanted to draw. It felt strange to be touched by his soft, cool hands.

'Yes.' Gabriel enthused. 'Look there, just like that.'

Relaxing back into her chair, Lucy allowed Gabriel to draw her.

* * *

It was strange to have someone look at you for so long. Flicking their eyes up and back. Wondering what they were doing but not being able to look. But Lucy didn't feel worried. It was Gabriel. There was no stress, no alarm. Just quiet-calm and the scratching of his pencils. He said he'd had work in the National Portrait Gallery when they'd first met. She'd never checked. It felt voyeuristic somehow.

After quite a long time, Gabriel said, 'I need my pastels, they're in the caravan. Don't move. I'll be right back.' He disappeared off outside, followed by the longing looks of the dogs.

Lucy desperately wanted to move, but she didn't want to spoil Gabriel's composition. So, she sat there, in the warm, by the fire, with her dogs, at peace and waiting for him to come back.

It was comforting to hear the door reopen and hear Gabriel return. Almost like a comforting security of predictability. Knowing someone said they were going to do something, and they did it.

Lucy felt at peace.

Excitedly, Gabriel returned to his seat, and opening his tin of pastel colours beside him on the chair, he started to flourish and colour the picture.

Lucy tried to let go of time.

'There. That's it. I have you.' Gabriel looked up happily from his work, and quickly grabbing another colour added a last highlight. Lucy didn't dare move. Was she allowed yet?

'Do you want to see?' Gabriel said, handing her her picture. 'Happy Christmas, Lucy. This is my present to you.'

Gabriel gently placed the picture on her lap. Lucy looked down at her likeness.

She looked beautiful.

The picture was quite incredible, somehow, and she couldn't quite tell how. He seemed to have the essence of her youth in the face of now, it was almost as if it was all of the different hers: the young and the naïve, the old and the weary, the reserved, the kind, the happy, the loving, all wrapped up in one picture. She had a gentle smile and the picture was a soft rainbow of colour. As if everything was lightly enhanced and pulled out for the world to see. It was an intimate picture, from someone that had seen into her soul and found it beautiful. For the first time in a very long time, Lucy didn't feel old and tired, she felt seen and beautiful.

Lucy tried to push back a little tear at the edge of her eye, as she looked down at her gift of beauty. She said, 'Thank you, Gabriel. This is an incredible gift. It is beautiful.'

Gabriel shook his head as he said, 'No Lucy. You are beautiful.' And kneeling beside her, he took her hand and respectfully kissed the back of it saying, 'Lucy, my light in the darkness.'

3. SPECIAL MULLED WINE

Bridget Bishop counted the pennies back into the jar, pursed her lips and clipped the lid closed. Sliding back into her favourite old chair by the fire, she set her mouth in a grim line. She tried to tuck in a stray grey hair by way of distraction. From behind her in the kitchen she heard the cat flap bounce and a skinny, black cat jumped up onto her lap, looking for love and attention.

'Old friend. You wanting some love? Some food? Come tell me.' said Bridget.

'Meow.' said the cat.

Bridget stroked the head of her long-time companion. 'Oh, little Lilith! We have a problem. I don't have enough money to see us through the winter, and you are so very fond of the most expensive cat food . . .'

Little Lilith pushed her head up against Bridget's hand in appreciation.

'So, Mummy is going to have to be a little creative.'

Lilith purred.

'What do you think if Mummy had a stall at the Christmas market? To sell some mulled wine, to keep people merry and full of Christmas cheer? Do you think that sounds good? Do you think we can make some money little one?'

Lilith blinked her yellow eyes at Bridget and Bridget looked back at her with her green ones, as the cat started to circle her lap, ready for her nap by the fire.

Bridget gently stroked the cat's little head with her fingers, then reaching out she pulled a book off the sideboard beside her, and read the title out loud to her companion: 'Gardener's Herbs and Their Uses. Volume One.' Lilith looked up and purred. Bridget continued, 'You see, my little friend, to make the best mulled wine you need to give it a kick, to make money you need to get people to drink more than one cup, and to drink more than one cup you need to give them a reason to stay and drink more. I can think of one very good reason why people want to stay at a bar and enjoy a drink – can't you my sweet?' Lilith didn't reply. Bridget stroked the warm, black, ball of fur on her lap, before skimming to page ninety-eight, whereupon she muttered to herself, 'Blue violets and red peppercorns, hum.'

The fire crackled merrily in the grate.

* * *

The Christmas market was in full swing, with the road running east beside the viaduct closed off to accommodate the wealth of Christmas stalls.

Bridget was situated right at the very end of the closed off road, the last in line, her sole ware displayed under a shabby, moth-eaten awning. She knew that the shoppers would be tired by the time they got to her, if they got to her at all. She was going to have to be her most charming and persuasive to get the customers in and keep them here.

Bridget surveyed her little, open tent. It had space for eight whiskey-barrel tables with associated cheap, metal, skinny, white, high stools. The main bar area, which was little more than some old tables pushed together, had a little, portable gas stove on top. On top of the gas stove was a massive saucepan of mulled wine, gently warming. Under the bar area tables were large plastic containers with more mulled wine ready to pour. This was where Bridget would be selling her "special" mulled wine from. Along the table, small, plastic cups were lined up, and there were boxes of spares under the table too.

Little fairy lights were gathered over the awning opening and festooned the ceiling of the tent. The lights twinkled against the damp, cold day; it was ten days before Christmas. In the background of the tent sat a little radio, the volume turned up as far as it would go, making its best effort to push Christmas songs out into the tent. Some potted basil plants (for prosperity) were dotted around here and there. Bridget had bought them using a very good offer of "two for one" at the supermarket. Deciding to maximise her earnings she'd bought ten. She could almost smell the coins filling her little jar already.

Letting out a deep sigh, Bridget felt ready. She stirred the mulled wine in the saucepan, over the dancing flames of the gas ring. Using a soup ladle, she carefully decanted the warm, spicy wine into some plastic cups and arranged them neatly on a tray. Then she wandered out under the awning with her tray of mulled wine, to tempt customers in.

At the other end of the Christmas market, she could see a crowd of busy shoppers clustering around brightly lit stalls of wooden tree decorations, knitted socks and stockings, and a large vat of *tartiflette*. Bridget shook her head. Knitting was far too much effort; the poor lady must have been knitting for months. Not Bridget's style. The *tartiflette* did smell nice though. Bridget sniffed the air hungrily. Not as nice as her special mulled wine she consoled herself. If only she could get her first customer . . .

A little way down the road, Bridget spied a sporty looking couple with matching rain jackets. Ah, she smiled to herself, they would do. Bridget muttered something under her breath. The lady from the couple looked up, and spying Bridget's tent, pointed to her companion. Slowly they made their way past the other stalls to Bridget's tent.

'Mulled wine my loves?' Bridget smiled warmly.

'Oh delicious!' the young lady said. 'How much?'

'A pound a cup.' Bridget neatly replied. The young

man twitched, but the young lady continued to smile kindly at Bridget.

'Of course. We'll take two.' Turning to her partner she smiled, 'Ken darling . . .'

Ken reluctantly reached into his pocket, brought out two coins and placed them onto the black-laced, fingerless-gloved palm of Bridget.

Bridget indicated to the sparse furniture inside the tent, 'Do sit down my dears, out of the draught and the cold winter air.'

Begrudgingly, Ken was led into the tent by his pretty companion, and he perched precariously on a thin, metal chair, to the beams and smiles of both women.

Bridget turned her attention back to the Christmas market before her. The crowd had migrated very slightly her way, however people were still getting stuck in clusters around the other stalls and that wouldn't do at all. Bridget muttered under her breath, and glancing back over shoulder smiled innocently to the young couple inside her tent. They were half-way through their cups already and talking together in a relaxed, easy manner. Bridget turned her attention back to the crowd at the end of the street, where a few people had broken away from the main huddle and were starting to wander her way. "Gently does it, Bridget dear." she said to herself.

An older man, with a younger, pretty, blonde-haired lady, approached Bridget and said, 'Mulled wine? I haven't had mulled wine in years. How much love?'

'A pound.' Bridget neatly replied.

'Two please.' The man answered, looking satisfied.

His young friend corrected him, 'One. I don't want a drink.'

Bridget turned to the young lady ensconced in her faux-fur hood and said, 'My special ingredient is blue violet, for its anti-wrinkle properties.' Winking she added, 'We all need a little lift at Christmas.'

The young lady shrugged and said to the man, 'Okay, I'll try one, Dave.'

Dave happily handed over the coins to Bridget's waiting, black-lace gloved hand. He guided his friend inside towards a skinny barrel table, where they perched precariously on the metal stools surrounding it.

Bridget pocketed the money and was soon greeted by a middle-aged couple. The lady was perhaps in her early forties, he was nearer fifty. It was hard to tell. Everyone looked young to Bridget.

Bridget greeted them, 'Mulled wine my loves?'

The lady giggled, 'Why not? Although just one because it's our first date.'

Bridget winked warmly at them. 'I'm sure this will take the edge off any first date nerves you have. Do take a drink and come inside.'

The lady giggled. Her red curls fell fetchingly around her face as she reached out her white, slim hand. Taking two drinks, and passing one to her date, she said, 'One for you, Barry. Do you mind where we sit?'

Barry shook his head, "No." and allowed himself to be dragged inside until Bridget gently held his arm. 'Two pounds.' she smiled and held out her black-lace gloved hand.

Barry pursed his lips, fished around in his pocket and pulled out two coins for her.

At that moment the young sporty lady from the first couple came up to Bridget and said, 'I'm so sorry to disturb you. My name is Emma. Your mulled wine is simply delicious, the best I've ever tried. Could Ken and I buy another cup?'

Bridget smiled at Emma warmly and nodded, saying, 'Oh, you warm an old lady's heart, what a kind thing to say, of course you can, my dear.' And passed the young sporty lady another two cups in exchange for two coins.

Bridget's tray was rapidly emptying and beside her another couple had arrived, with a few more couples slowly weaving their way to her from behind this couple. Bridget smiled warmly as she said, 'Mulled wine my loves?'

The couple nodded in agreement as they emptied the tray and Bridget led them inside, under the tent awning.

As Bridget headed towards her little bar area, she noticed Ken move his skinny stool a little closer to Emma's. Bridget tried to disguise a smile and look busy as she refilled the tray of drinks. She only just made it back to the entrance of the tent to greet another three couples, before Dave approached her for two more cups. Apparently, Fabienne was quite convinced of the anti-aging properties of the blue violet special ingredient, and he had been instructed to get some more. Dave's face was flushed and he looked happy. Carrying back the cups, Bridget noticed him slip his hand up under the back of Fabienne's jacket as he sat down. Fabienne seemed to quite welcome the move and flashed him one of her rare, pretty smiles.

Bridget hardly had time to register the happy couple before some more patrons arrived to buy her mulled wine, and come into the small, moth-eaten tent, adorned with fairy lights and humming out Christmas songs.

* * *

The tent was full.

Customers had filled the stools, the spaces between the stools, and were starting to spill out onto the market road outside. The fairy lights were twinkling prettily against the fading light of the day. The market may have started with a crowd at the front end, but the critical mass had moved, and there were more people at Bridget's end of the road than anywhere else. Even the man from the *tartiflette* van had time to come out from his van, look around and scratch his head as he took in the crowd at the end of the road.

The tent was not only full, but with so many

patrons huddled together on this crisp cooling evening, it was starting to get steamy. Bodies were moving past each other with just centimetres to spare, people were shimmying past crowds to get to the bar area, where Bridget was trying to keep up with the orders for her delicious "special" mulled wine. She barely had time to take in the bubbling throng of happy people, she almost missed Dave cornered at the edge of the tent, wrapped up in the arms and faux-fur of a passionate kiss from Fabienne.

The lady on her first date, with the lovely curly, red hair, faced Bridget from across the "bar". She was almost scrunching her body with excitement as she said, 'Oh another two cups please and be quick. This is quite simply the best first date I've ever had.'

Bridget hurried about her task, carefully pouring the warm liquid into the little plastic cups. Smiling, she handed the cups to the young lady in exchange for two coins, as the young lady confessed to her, 'He just asked me my opinion on people who get engaged when they've just met, and what I thought about love at first sight. I mean. Have you ever heard of a guy voluntarily talking about such things?' Bridget was lost for words as the young lady raised her eyebrows at her and proclaimed, 'Exactly.' Excitedly spinning around, she rushed off to where Barry had kept her seat at a coveted table.

Two more men came forward to claim some

drinks.

❋ ❋ ❋

Sarah Yelland, head of midwifery at the maternity unit at Stracathro Hospital, tapped the numbers into the computer and rubbed her forehead. This couldn't be right. One of the girls must have got the numbers mixed up or put them in the wrong way around. Probably Poppy, that girl was always annoying her (Poppy was Sarah Yelland's favourite scapegoat).

Huffing, Sarah locked her computer, grabbed her coffee cup, and went to see if she could have a word with Poppy. Catching a colleague in the staff room she found that unfortunately she couldn't speak to Poppy right now as she was in the middle of delivering a baby in the water bath. How annoying. Little daffodils hit their heads against the windowpane, laughing at Sarah from their prison outside in the flower box on the windowsill. Instead, Sarah turned to her next favourite scapegoat, Mary, and demanded to know where the error had come from.

'No error.' Mary replied.

Sarah barked back, 'Well there must be. September is usually four hundred births for the whole month, give or take a little. We are only in late March and we already have two hundred births registered for the weekend of the 10 September alone. I'm sorry, but if this is a joke, then it's not a very funny one.'

Mary replied, 'No error, and not a jo—.'

'Got another one!' Casey burst into the staff room waving an ultrasound in the air.

Sarah whipped around to face the staff room door and Casey quickly composed herself. Sarah narrowed her eyes and said suspiciously, 'Another one, what?'

Casey swallowed hard. 'Erm. Another due date for early September. Looks like the date of the ninth, give or take a few days.'

'Is this some kind of trick?' Sarah snapped.

Casey indicated to the corridor behind her. 'They're just in the corridor behind me, see for yourself.'

Sarah yanked back the door and poked her head out suspiciously. There she saw a couple, a lady with curly, red hair, and a man beside her who was carefully guiding the lady, with his arm around the back of her waist, out of the maternity unit. The couple walked slowly, gazing at the small black and white ultrasound picture in the lady's hands. Another three couples were waiting by reception, they'd ran out of chairs so the men had to stand, looking awkward.

Sarah firmly shut the door and turned back to her midwives, whose smiles hastily fell from their faces.

This was turning out to be a very bad day.

* * *

In one of the little villages about ten miles past the outskirts of the city, Bridget admired her new camper van. Holding Lilith in her arms and circling it, she said, 'Well my dear, are you ready for an adventure? We are going to have a little holiday south, around some woodlands. We're going to pick some blue violets. What do you think about that my sweet?'

Lilith nuzzled her head up under her owner's chin and purred happily. Quite frankly, Lilith had never eaten so well as the last few months. Bridget could take her anywhere she wanted, as long as she kept supplying her with such delicious food. Really, hunting was such a bore. Lilith happily nuzzled her owner again.

* * *

Bridget lit the fire and sat down heavily in her favourite comfy chair. The last of the September warmth was leaving and soon the cold winter winds would be on their way. It was so lovely to have the fire blazing away, warming her toes.

Straightening out the newspaper on her lap, Bridget read aloud to her cat: 'Bumper Year for a Baby Boom. Stracathro Hospital has successfully survived a mini baby boom with a record nine-hundred and twelve babies in the month of September, four hundred and fifty of which were born over the weekend of 10 September. Extra midwives from the surrounding area and specialist cross-trained nurses from other disciplines had to be deployed, in what is being described as, a mini baby boom for the area. Head Midwife, Sarah Yelland, gave a statement yesterday saying . . .'

Bridget put down the paper and looked down at the fireside mat, where Lilith was curled up by her feet.

'Did you ever hear of such a thing, Lilith? Mini baby boom.' Bridget clicked her tongue at the salacious gossip, as Lilith raised her head slightly from her cosy curl and smiled up at her owner. Bridget continued, 'On a different note, my sweet, I may need to switch to the cheaper cat food.' Lilith raised an eyebrow in annoyance. 'I'm so sorry dear puss.' Bridget raised her eyes to the coin jar on the mantlepiece, then shifting her bottom slightly in the chair she removed a new, fancy, slim, pink mobile phone from her cardigan pocket and swiped for her banking app. Bridget clicked her tongue again as she surveyed the balance and shook her head. 'I think, dear cat,' and Bridget paused as she firmed up the idea, 'I think we might need to do another Christmas market stall this year. What do you think about that?'

Lilith smiled and nuzzled her head back into her paws in front of the warm fire.

4. CHRISTMAS TELEVISION

Ricky stomped in through the door of their flat and shivered with the cold. From the living room Emma called, 'Did you manage to top up the electric?'

'Yes!' Ricky called back triumphantly.

It was Christmas Eve and bitterly cold outside in the city of Dundee, where temperatures had already dropped below freezing. Ricky kicked off his boots and hung up his jacket, damp from the snow, on the coat hook. He also took off his damp hat and scarf, then put on a dry woolly hat and a big all-in-one fleece, which engulfed his skinny body. Coming through to the living room, he joined Emma on the sofa under the duvet, which was wrapped around her as she sat watching the TV.

'Oh! You're cold.' she said.

'Can I still have a kiss for topping up the electric?' Ricky replied.

Emma reached up her lips to his and said, 'Always. You can have all my kisses.' Their eyes rested on each other. No matter how tough times got, they always had each other, and they always would. 'Thank you, my hero.' Emma said with love in her eyes.

Ricky reached his thin arm around her and pulled her close. He loved the scent of her. Her natural scent, not perfumes or deodorant. It worried him that they were both getting skinny, but he tried not to show it. They just had to get through this winter, he'd get a better job and everything would be all right.

Ricky looked at Emma's sleek, straight hair. The blonde tideline was now at her ears with a wave of dark brunette following it. He didn't care. It looked kind of cool actually. Besides, she'd always be beautiful to him: her pale skin, sharp nose, big lobed ears and pale blue eyes. He loved every quirk about her and she loved him, despite his hawkish nose and thin, black, greasy hair; despite his non-descript dark-brown eyes. She always looked at him like he was a hero, and for that he'd do anything to keep her happy.

Times were tough though. Ricky pushed back the feeling of panic and sick rising from his stomach and clutched her a little tighter. One day they'd look back on these difficult times and laugh.

Emma reached over to the side of the sofa and passed Ricky a tea she'd made for him just before he came in. Gratefully he received it and hugged the warmth of the mug to him.

'I've not put in milk.' Emma said. 'I thought I'd save it for tomorrow. For Christmas Day. If that's okay?'

'Yep. Absolutely.' Proudly, Ricky added, 'I put fifteen pounds on the electric. It should see us through today, tomorrow and on into Boxing Day. I think my mum is going to drop off some money tomorrow in my card for Christmas, so we can use it to top up the electric after that.'

Emma snuggled a little closer to Ricky under the duvet on the sofa, and lifting the TV controls out from underneath her, she said, 'Anything you fancy watching?'

'*Homes for Auction*? *Treasure in the Attic*?' he suggested. Ricky watched as Emma pointed the controller at the TV and found something suitable. Out of the corner of his eye he could see the electric heater sitting cold and idle, but he tried to ignore it. Just as he tried to ignore the damp, peeling, lining paper and the bare floorboards. He knew he could do these jobs, he was perfectly able to repaint or lay some carpet, they just had to be able to buy the paint or the carpet first. Not this winter. Maybe next year.

Cuddled up together under the duvet, Ricky and Emma quietly watched TV, as the hours towards Christmas slipped by.

* * *

Christmas morning was full of surprises. Emma had bought some slippers for Ricky and, with much hilarity and laughing, Ricky presented Emma with a pair too.

Ricky laughed as Emma hit him with a pink,

fluffy, slipper-boot. He said, 'How was I to know you'd bought the same? We think too alike. At least we'll have warm feet.'

Emma poked her tongue out. She was actually rather pleased with her slippers and it was quite funny. One for the memory box.

Emma got up to make some buttered toast for them for breakfast. Ricky watched her padded, fleeced-covered shape leave the bedroom with a little tear in his eye. Then, jumping up, he reached under the bed mattress (the bed was the only item of furniture in the room so the only good hiding place) and pulled out a little leather box. Carefully opening it, he checked the contents were still safely inside. From inside the box twinkled a tiny blue sapphire stone on a skinny gold ring band.

Ricky's mum had said that she was ok to give her engagement ring to Ricky, as she could see how in love he and Emma were, and she wanted Ricky to do the right thing by Emma. Ricky had passed his mum fifty pounds for it. All his savings. But it would be worth it. He was as excited as a kid on Christmas Eve waiting for Santa. He knew Emma would love it. Quickly hiding the box back under the mattress, he decided that he'd pop the question after lunch.

* * *

Lunch was a simple affair. It was toast again, with baked beans and a tin of stewing steak that Emma had been saving back. They'd also been given a box of mince pies from the foodbank, so they finished with a mince pie each, and decided to save two more for that night and have the last two tomorrow.

Feeling happy and content, with cosy feet and hearts full of love, they wandered back through to the living room, to cuddle up together on the sofa and watch an afternoon of Christmas TV under the duvet.

Ricky decided to put the electric heater on for half an hour, while Emma searched the TV guide for something she wanted to watch. Feeling that this was the right moment (as they were full of food and love, and warm air was filling the damp, cold room) Ricky nipped through to the bedroom. Coming back, he slipped under the duvet with Emma. Gently, he took the TV controls from her, pressed "mute" and said:

'Emma?'

Emma turned and looked at him strangely, she had just about decided what she wanted to watch, she wanted the TV controls back.

'Yes?' Emma said, looking at Ricky with puzzled eyes.

Ricky leant forward and kissed her nose. He had tears in his eyes when he said, 'From the moment I met you at school I knew you were the one. I knew we would always be together. There is no other woman for me. You are perfect.'

Emma looked teary, and wrapping her arms

around him, said, 'You big softie. You know I love you.'

Ricky replied, 'I know you do, which is why, I wanted to ask you . . . will you be my wife?' Out from his cargo-trouser pocket and up under the duvet, Ricky produced a little, battered, leather ring box.

Emma clamped her hand over her mouth in shock.

Ricky continued, 'Emma, will you marry me?' He carefully opened the box, so that the ring wouldn't fall out. The slightly worn, skinny ring, glittered at Emma from inside the box. Carefully, he took the ring out, then reaching for Emma's left hand he placed the ring on her finger. Amazingly, it wasn't a bad fit for size, a little loose, but nothing that couldn't be fixed when they had the money.

Tears were streaming down Emma's face as she said, 'Yes!' then clasping her arms around Ricky's neck, she squeezed him tight and said, 'I love you so much.'

'I love you too.' said Ricky. Then added, 'I'm sorry it's not a new ring. It was Mum's engagement ring, and now that Dad has been dead ten years, she said she'd rather you had it. I hope that's okay.'

Emma looked proudly down at the ring on her hand and said, 'Ricky, it is the most beautiful ring I've ever seen.' Again, wrapping her arms around him and covering him with kisses she said, 'I love you so much.'

Ricky had never felt so happy. They rang Emma's

dad, and then her mum and stepdad with the good news. After that they rang Ricky's mum, who congratulated them. It seemed that unfortunately one of Ricky's mum's neighbours had had a break-in the night before and Ricky's mum was helping them sort the damage and trying to get the police out. She apologised that she wouldn't pop over today but promised to see them tomorrow.

With all the phone calls and good wishes out of the way, Emma left for the kitchen to wind a bit of cotton thread around the engagement ring band, to stop it slipping off. Ricky was left with the TV controls to find something for them to watch.

Clicking off the electric heater, Ricky jumped back under the duvet and pointed the controls at the TV. Emma quite liked reality TV programmes, so he flicked to "celebrity reality 24" to see what was on offer.

Three p.m. *Ricky and Emma's Wedding.*

Ricky did a double take. No way. There was a celebrity couple with exactly the same names as them. Okay, Richard and Emma weren't that uncommon as Christian names. But still. Ricky read the programme information:

> *Follow Ricky and Emma, a celebrity couple who met on the set of* Jungle Adventure. *Watch Ricky propose to Emma and see them plan their extravagant Christmas themed wedding . . .*

What were the chances that this celebrity couple

had the same name, and that the programme was about getting engaged! Ricky clicked it on, knowing that Emma would really love this.

Emma came back into the living room and shut the door to try and keep in the last of the heat. 'What's this?' she asked, pointing at the TV and snuggling up with Ricky under the duvet. Happily, she took out her hand with the engagement ring, flashed it at him, gave him a kiss and turned her attention back to the TV.

'You'll never believe it, but it's about a celebrity couple with the same names as us, who have just got engaged!' Ricky said.

'Huh! What are the chances?' said Emma. 'Can I just say. We were there first.' And proudly took another look at her ring before slipping it back under the duvet.

Outside the flat window the light started to drop. Inside the flat the temperature started to drop too now that the electric fire was off. It was forecast to be a cold night tonight, possibly down to minus ten. But Emma and Ricky were quite cosy under their duvet and their hearts were warm with love. In front of them a riot of glorious colour entertained them as they sat to watch a couple just like them.

The programme started with an opening scene of a large, white, Surrey farmhouse, surrounded with paddocks and two horses grazing on hay at the edge of the field. Emma (the celebrity) was rubbing one of the horse's noses. The presenter asked her,

'So tell me about the moment you knew Ricky was the one.'

'Well,' Celebrity Emma replied. I think it was when he was covered in spiders during one of the jungle trials. I just hate spiders.' she shuddered.

In the little flat in Dundee, Emma shuddered too, and turned to Ricky saying, 'Oh my goodness. I hate spiders too!' Ricky smiled at her and pulled her closer to him as they turned their attention back to the TV.

Celebrity Emma continued, 'He just seemed so brave to me. A real hero. I think that's the moment I fell in love.'

The programme cut to Celebrity Ricky in the farmhouse's large double garage, polishing one of his motorbikes. The presenter asked, 'Ricky, how did you know Emma was the one?'

Celebrity Ricky put down the rag and placed his hand on his motorbike to stand up. He gave the question his full attention. 'It was her eyes. The first time I saw those baby blues I just knew.' Celebrity Ricky looked down at his feet, and discretely wiped a tear away from the side of his eye, trying to avoid the glare of the rolling camera.

The presenter continued, 'So you want to make the engagement quite special?'

'Yes, I do.' he replied. 'Which is why I wanted to have this as a documentary. I want every moment of our journey to be remembered. We started on TV, I'm going to propose on TV,' laughing he added, 'We'll probably die on TV. Ha ha.'

The presenter asked, 'Can you show us the ring?'

'Yeah.' Celebrity Ricky replied, and from his cargo-trouser pocket her pulled out a little, blue, leather box. Flicking it open and holding it for the camera man to see, he said, 'My mum had a sapphire engagement ring and she loved my dad a lot. So, I wanted one just like it. Only nice and big. Because I love Emma a lot.'

Inside the little leather box, nestled the most enormous sapphire gemstone flanked by two pear-shaped diamonds, sparkling in the halogen lights of the double garage.

The presenter said, 'It's a beautiful ring. Are you nervous about proposing tomorrow? What if she says no?'

Celebrity Ricky looked into the camera with all seriousness. 'I know her better than I know my-self. She won't say "No." because we're soul mates and we're destined to be together, if not in this life, then in the next.'

The presenter asked, 'Do you believe in reincarnation, Ricky?'

'Yeah.' Celebrity Ricky replied. 'I've been on a Buddhist retreat. I've really tried to embrace density and fate. I really think there is something in it. Don't you?'

From under the duvet on the sofa, Emma pulled out her ring again and said to Ricky, 'Isn't that amazing? He got her a sapphire too.' Emma didn't want to make Ricky embarrassed though, so she added, 'But mine is a lot better, because it is an antique and it has meaning.'

Ricky lovingly looked at Emma in the darkness, highlighted by the glow of the TV, and kissed her forehead as he said, 'What ever did I do to deserve you?'

They snuggled together a little closer as the programme cut to a scene in Celebrity Emma and Ricky's kitchen.

It was an enormous farmhouse kitchen, with creamy-coloured, limestone flagstones; thick, white shaker cabinets; sparkly stone worktops in white marble; a large, double oven and a huge central kitchen island. Celebrity Emma was sitting on a bar stool at the kitchen island as Celebrity Ricky cooked dinner for them both, behind her.

In their cold Dundee living room Emma and Ricky could almost smell the eggs and bacon cooking. *Mmm.* Around them in the flat, the last of the light and the heat escaped. Ricky and Emma were completely absorbed by the TV programme, and hardly noticed as they shivered together under the thin duvet.

From behind the camera, the presenter asked Celebrity Emma about their life together as boyfriend and girlfriend. 'So, Emma, you've had some high-profile boyfriends and some painful break-ups. How do you feel about moving in with Ricky so quickly?'

Celebrity Emma gulped, took a quick sip of her white wine in a large, sleek glass, and said, 'This time it just feels different. I just know. Every part of me knows.' And looking over to Celebrity Ricky cooking behind her in the kitchen she said, 'Plus he can cook!'

From behind her, Celebrity Ricky raised his arm and waved the spatula at the camera crew to prove the point. Then turning and flashing a smile at his girlfriend he gave her a wink.

Celebrity Emma smiled, flicked back her perfect, blonde-highlighted hair and continued, 'It's like I've met him before somehow. Honestly,' Celebrity Emma looked directly at the camera and said, 'I'd rather spend a hundred lifetimes just with Ricky than one lifetime without him.'

The presenter asked her, 'Do you think you'll get married and have kids?'

'Absolutely.' Celebrity Emma replied, 'When he asks me.'

From behind Celebrity Emma, Celebrity Ricky turned around and gave a secret wink at the rolling camera.

'Cut!' Shouted the camera man.

'Great.' The presenter replied, and addressing Ricky and Emma said, 'I think we've got all we need for today. We'll be back tomorrow at nine a.m. sharp, so just make sure that the hair and makeup teams have finished by then.'

Emma drained the last of her wine as Ricky started to serve up dinner. 'Anyone else for bacon, egg and chips?' Ricky asked, turning around the camera man, sound man and presenter. But everyone was a "No." They were all eager to get back to their families for the night.

Emma got up from the kitchen island and walked past the TV crew to get a wine refill from the fridge. 'Ouch!' she said, stopping suddenly at the end of the kitchen and rubbing her head. She looked up puzzled.

Ricky turned around from his cooking and looked over in concern at Emma. 'You okay?' he asked.

Emma placed her hand out in front of her, almost as if she was touching an invisible wall. 'Ricky,' she said, 'There's something strange going on here. I can't get to the other end of the kitchen.'

Ricky came over still holding the spatula. In-specting her head, he then reached out his hands to the glass wall that seemed to be preventing them from reaching the other end of their kitchen. Behind them were the sounds of the TV crew pack-ing up.

'That's really odd.' he said.

Behind him the camera man said to the sound engineer, 'Okay, just the camera spotlights to turn off.'

The kitchen was plunged into darkness.

* * *

On a freezing Christmas night, in the city of Dun-dee, the electricity meter in a small, damp flat clicked empty.

In the living room, the TV switched off next to an

unused electric fire. On the sofa a young couple lay wrapped in each other's arms, huddling together for warmth. Their lips were blue with hypothermia and their mouths exhaled their last breaths, as their souls left their bodies, to find each other in another lifetime.

5. RETREAT, RECHARGE, RELOVE

Lucille stood in front of the charming wooden A-frame lodge and exhaled. The guide who had accompanied her on his snowmobile, turned off his engine and similarly stood to look at the deep-golden wooden lodge, covered in snow; nestled amongst green, spiky, snow-covered pine trees. He then looked over at his guest.

Far from the first flushes of youth; she was well presented and clearly took care of herself. She had short, styled, honey-blonde hair and enchanting grey eyes, topped by thick, false lashes. Her brow also seemed surprisingly smooth compared to her neck and she wore expensive cashmeres and faux-furs. From her emanated a distinctive chocolate-vanilla smelling perfume. He was used to the look and the smell of money. The lady was of average height, slim and toned. She was similar to one of a hundred women that he'd escorted here over the years. But the fact that she was here for Christmas and was planning to spend it alone meant that there was some sadness working its way through. He shrugged, most people came here to get lost and find themselves again. Some stayed lost even when they returned home. None of his business.

Addressing her, the guide asked, 'Do you want me to unlock the lodge and take the bags in?'

Drawing her eyes away from the perfectly charming wooden lodge, Lucille smiled gratefully at the guide. 'Thank you so much. That would be wonderful.' she said.

Unpacking his guest's bags and lifting the packages of food shopping off the snowmobile sled, the guide directed Lucille to the lodge and showed her how to unlock the door. 'I'll just be five minutes bringing this in and then I'll light the fire for you.' he said.

'Oh, no rush,' Lucille graciously replied. 'It seems quite warm in here.'

'Yes, that's from our site generated renewable energy, which is stored in batteries and powering the underfloor heating. We also have generators (for backup). There are solar panels and wind turbines further up the valley. You've probably already seen that on the website? But it's always nice to have a cosy fire too. You'll find the lodge has been built with the highest eco-certifications and eco-friendly insulation. It'll be quite warm. But as I said earlier. I'm on call. Any problems just call my mobile.' the guide concluded.

'Thank you.' Lucille said again. She unwound her scarf and started to wander around the lodge retreat where she would be spending the next two weeks. She'd wanted to get away from it all, and here she really would. No cheating men. No gold-digging women. Just her and her thoughts. She even thought about trying to write some poetry – but it had been so long. The family had been a little upset about her wanting to spend Christmas alone, but after everything that had happened, she really needed time out to put herself first, and think about what she wanted and where she was going.

Once the guide had finished taking her bags upstairs, and unpacking the food away in the open plan kitchen, he showed Lucille around.

The downstairs was a large open plan area. The living area was at the front of the lodge and open to the dining area and kitchen at the back. Between the living area and the dining area was a large, dual-aspect, modern wood burner, large enough to warm the entire downstairs space. Soft, beige, velvet sofas in the living area, were generously covered with white, faux-fur throws, in compliment to the little faux-sheepskin throws that were placed over the rustic wooden benches, either side of the rustic wooden table in the dining area. The kitchen was made from the same rich wood that was used to construct the lodge. From both the front and the back of the lodge, large, triple-glazed, floor to ceiling windows, looked out onto the snow-covered landscape all around. From the back windows, in the distance, Lucille could just about make out another A-frame lodge. It was clearly part of this small holiday hamlet, but it was far enough away not to bother her. She could also see on the decking behind the lodge, a hot tub festooned with fairy lights.

At the side of the open plan area, and rising up over the kitchen, some open-stepped, wooden stairs took Lucille upstairs to the bedroom. There was a large, king-sized bed, covered with an intricate red-and-white, handmade, patchwork counterpane. The upstairs space also had views to the front and back of the lodge. Over the stairs a large bathroom area was panelled off. It contained a jacuzzi bath, sauna and two sparkling marble sinks, perched on top of a wooden cupboard.

Every aspect of the lodge was warm and welcoming. Lucille let out a deep sigh as she felt herself start to unwind. This was just what she needed.

The guide instructed her that the wood for the fire was stored to the side of the house, but either he or the cleaners will be in daily to bring it in for her. He handed her the lodge keys and said, 'I'll be back tomorrow morning to top-up the wood in the baskets downstairs. If you change your mind about doing your own cooking, we do have a chef available to cook meals.'

'Thank you so much. I appreciate your time. No, I think I'd like to cook for myself and just take some time out alone. But thank you though. I appreciate it.' Lucille replied.

'No problem. The cleaners are in daily between approximately nine and ten a.m. They have a spare key, so don't worry if you are out and about. Text me if there is anything specific that you need.' he said.

Lucille smiled her thanks and saw the helpful guide out. She watched as he pushed her snowmobile up to the house, and waving, was off, whizzing down the slopes, no doubt to settle in another visitor in one of the other nine lodges dotted around the area. Not that you'd know. Apart from the lodge just visible behind this one, she hadn't seen any of the other lodges when she came up hill.

Lucille warmed herself in front of the fire while sipping a large glass of red wine. She read the welcome pack and looked at the mapped paths for some of the suggested walks around the area, she also had the snowmobile if she wanted to go a little further. But this evening she just wanted to unwind, have a bath, and try to forget about the last few weeks.

* * *

Lucille slept in late the next morning and was still in her faux-fur all-in-one, drinking a coffee machine tab cappuccino, and looking out at the view, when the cleaners arrived. The guide had already been in while she'd been having her lie-in to top up the firewood. It was a lazy start to the day but it had been bliss not to rush.

After the cleaners left, Lucille decided to do some gentle yoga on the mat in front of the fire. She'd just finished her practice, when to her horror, she saw a man with a camera taking pictures of her, from outside the lodge.

Swearing, Lucille rushed upstairs and peered out at him from behind some furniture. There he was again! In front of the lodge, as bold as brass. *Snap, snap, snap.* The man was well-wrapped up against the cold in his padded snow jacket and trousers. From under his red, wool hat she could see his shoulder-length, dark-brown hair with a slight wave. He held a very posh looking camera. The man couldn't be more than thirty.

Lucille watched as he circled around the lodge to the back, where he took a few more pictures. Finishing up and putting his camera away, he made a beeline for the lodge in the distance behind hers.

Lucille was quite shaken up and dithered for a minute deciding what to do. Should she call the guide and report it? Should she ignore it? "No." she resolved, she'd had enough of being dependent on men and letting men scare her into ignoring their bad behaviour. No, she wasn't having this. She wasn't going to have her retreat spoilt by him or anyone else. She needed clear boundaries and taking photos of her wasn't okay. She would go right up to the other lodge now and sort this man out.

Running high on adrenaline, Lucille hastily dressed for the cold and the snow outside, and stomping with anger, she retraced the man's footprints in the snow up to his lodge. It was a bit further to walk than she realised, it was also hard work stomping up through the snow. By the time she reached the lodge she was a little tired physically, but her anger drove her on. She stood panting in front of the wooden lodge. It was an exact replica of the one she was staying in.

Bang. Bang. Bang.

Lucille hammered on the lodge door. She thought she heard the man moving around inside, and she prepared herself for what she would say. If he got nasty then, well, maybe she'd just have to get nasty too.

The door slowly opened and a kind-looking, pair of blue eyes looked out, framed by a tanned face, a neatly trimmed, dark-brown beard, and a head of wavy, dark-brown hair, which fell to the man's shoulders. He looked about thirty. He was wearing a thick, red-checked, brushed-cotton shirt; jeans and thick, green, woollen socks. He was about six feet tall. In his hand he held a cereal bowl and appeared to be part way through his morning snack.

'Hello?' The man said uncertainly. 'Can I help you?'

Suddenly, Lucille's anger started to evaporate. He seemed quite nice. He didn't really look like a stalker. Still. Lucille needed to set some boundaries. Bluntly, she said, 'Stop taking photos of me.'

The man nearly chocked on his cereal. 'I'm sorry?' he said.

'I said. Stop taking photos of me.'

'But I haven't been.' The man protested.

Lucille started to feel rather uncertain of herself. He seemed quite sure. Perhaps it was another man? But there was no one else around and this looked like the man she'd seen from the upstairs window. Lucille continued, 'I watched you, not more than twenty minutes ago, outside my lodge, taking photos of me through the windows.'

The man protested his innocence. 'Honestly, I wasn't taking photos of you. I was taking photos of the lodges. It's my job. I can't take photos of you through the windows anyway, as it's special glass. See.' He pointed to the huge windows crammed into the apex of his lodge. 'Look.' he said pointing. 'Can you see in?'

Lucille realized she couldn't and started to feel like she'd just made a very embarrassing mistake.

The man continued, 'Right, but check this out.' Grabbing Lucille by the hand, he pulled her through into the lodge to see the reality on the other side.

The lodge had the same layout as the one she was staying in, but what a difference! It was a mess. On the table sat camera with associated accessories, some discarded clothing was lying on the sofa, and there appeared to be a plate with the remains of last night's dinner still stuck to it. Didn't the cleaners visit here? She certainly hadn't seen all this through the window.

'Oh!' Lucille said. She shook her gloved hand free from his.

'You see?' the guy said. 'I wasn't looking at you or taking photos of you, because I couldn't see you. As I said. I was just taking photos of the lodge.'

Lucille turned to look at him quizzically. 'What

exactly is it that you do?' she asked.

Proudly the man replied, 'I'm an influencer. I take photos of remote locations. A sort of "Wish you were here?" idea. I can show you my Instagram and Facebook pages?'

Before Lucille could protest, he placed his bowl on the coffee table, closed the door, whipped his phone out of his back pocket and started scrolling through pages and pages of beautiful photos. He was close enough that she could smell his fresh pine shower gel scent. Lucille tried not to think about it.

There were pictures of woodlands, forest re-treats, campfires, people canoeing, outdoor parties of people under fairy lights. It looked lovely and the photos really were rather good. Lucille flicked a look at the man's camera on the table. It seemed like she'd made a terrible mistake.

Blushing deep-red, Lucille said, 'I'm so terribly sorry. I didn't realise. I thought you were taking pictures of me. I hate it when . . . that is . . . it's been . . . well, I've been through . . . '

The kind man stopped scrolling through his phone and placed his hand on her arm, saying, 'Hey. It's okay. I'm made of tougher stuff than get-ting flustered by a feisty female.'

Lucille blushed even harder.

The man continued, 'My name's Oliver. What's yours?' He held out his hand.

Lucille took off her glove and placed her hand in-side his. 'I'm Lucille.' she said quietly. Honestly, she just wished the ground would eat her up. She was so embarrassed.

'Would you like to stay for a coffee or something now that you're here? Have a chat?' Oliver asked.

Part of Lucille did want to talk to someone about everything that had happened to her the past few weeks, but not to this guy and not after what had just happened and the way she'd behaved. Lucille just wanted to get out of here as soon as possible and bury her face in a pillow.

Lucille replied, 'Err. Thank you. No. I've got something I need to get back to.' Outside the window the trees swayed gently in the morning breeze, and a calm stillness settled over the valley. 'Err. That is. Something I'm doing. I . . . err, I've got to go.'

'What is it that you're doing?' Oliver asked.

Lucille said the first thing that came into her head. 'Poetry. I'm in the middle of a poem. I need to get back to it.'

'Poetry? That's cool. I'd love to hear some of your poems sometime. That is if you're not still mad at me?'

'Not mad. So sorry. My mistake. Got to go.' Lucille hastily pulled her glove back on and turned for the door.

Touching Lucille on the arm again, Oliver said, 'Hey, perhaps you'd like to do dinner sometime? I cook a great steak, and we are neighbours for a short while. It's nearly Christmas.'

Lucille smiled politely thinking of the mess on

the coffee table and wondering exactly what state the kitchen would be in. Graciously, she said, 'Oh, yes. Absolutely. I'd love that. Right. Got to go. Bye.' Releasing the door handle, she rushed out of the front door, desperate to get back to her lodge and away from this cringeworthy situation.

* * *

By the time evening came around, Lucille found she'd nearly got over her embarrassment and was *almost* able to look back at the incident this morning and laugh. Almost.

Lucille decided that she needed to unwind and chill out. So, she turned the outside hot tub on, changed in to her bikini, wrapped herself in a very thick dressing gown, and with her glass of champagne tightly in her hand, slipped into the lovely hot water.

The hot tub on the deck was surrounded by fairy lights, stars and gently swaying trees. This was bliss and just what Lucille needed.

Lucille rested back in the warm, bubbling water. She could feel all her stress and cares drifting away. She felt lighter and happier. Almost as if she was beginning to connect to the girl she used to be: the carefree romantic. The girl that existed before her traumas of lies, cheating and broken hearts.

Although the last few weeks had been awful, they hadn't been entirely unexpected. In truth, Lucille had been in a bad situation for a long time.

She had the perspective now to see that.

Lucille wanted to reconnect to the Lucille before. Who she really was. She used to sing all the time when she was younger. She hadn't sung for years. Lucille tried to remember some of the love songs she'd used to sing with her mum in the kitchen when she was growing up. Lucille sipped her champagne under the starlit sky and started to sing to herself.

A voice came out from the darkness beyond her decking, 'Hey, great voice!'

Lucille swore, turned around and placed her hand over her chest.

Oliver came a few steps up the decking into the light. 'Hot tub. Great idea. That looks nice.'

Lucille did a double take. Was he asking to come in? She tried to rein herself in. She'd already embarrassed herself by being indignant before to him. She didn't want to dig herself in deeper.

'Err. Thanks.' Lucille said uncertainly, as she dipped her body further down into the water.

Oliver seemed to hesitate. 'I . . . err. Well. I'll let you get back to it then.' He was just about to turn to walk back down the steps when he lifted his camera into the air and said, 'Just so you know, I wasn't taking photos of you.' He looked wistfully up at Lucille in the hot tub, 'Although, I think that would be a great photo by the way.' He turned away and started to walk down the steps as he called back at her from the darkness beyond. 'By the way, dinner at mine, tomorrow. Seven p.m. Don't be late. Hope you like steak.' And he was gone.

Lucille sat in the warm water, stunned, clutching her half-full glass of champagne. He hadn't even waited for her to say yes. He'd just assumed.

* * *

Lucille stood in front of the wardrobe in the bright morning-light and wondered what to wear. She did have two wool jumper dresses, but she'd be walking between lodges, and getting wet, cold legs wasn't clever. It would have to be jeans and a jumper. If she did the white jeans with the thick-knit, cream, Bardot-style jumper and her diamond drop earrings, then that could still look classy for dinner?

With her outfit for the evening decided, Lucille relaxed by the fire, painted her nails, got herself another machine tab cappuccino and considered her next problem.

Lucille had told Oliver yesterday that she was a poet. That she wrote poetry. Well, yes, she did a long time ago, but she hadn't written any in years, and from the little she knew of this man, he would almost certainly ask her to read some to him.

Snuggling up in her faux-fur all-in-one, in front of the fire, and overlooking the beautiful views from the living room window, Lucille picked up the new, pale-green, moleskin-covered notebook and sleek Parker pen, and started to write. She'd need at least five or six poems by tonight if she wasn't going to look completely ridiculous. Again.

* * *

At seven p.m. sharp, Lucille knocked on Oliver's lodge door. She felt silly. She hardly even knew the guy, but she did feel like she owed him an apology, and at least this seemed to be going a little way towards that. Also she did feel a bit self-conscious that he'd seen her in her bikini in the hot tub yesterday. She guessed she was older than him by at least ten years. He said he hadn't looked. Hadn't he?

Lucille's thoughts were whirring as Oliver pulled open the door.

Oliver's hair was slightly dishevelled. He wore another checked shirt. This time blue. Again, blue jeans. He had a tea towel thrown over his shoulder and a cooking spatula in his hand. His shirt sleeves were rolled up, revealing his muscly arms.

'Hi Lucille!' Oliver said with a big wide smile. 'Come in!' He ushered her through to the living room with a guiding arm behind her back. 'Here,' he said, putting the spatula and tea towel briefly down on the sideboard, 'Let me help you with your things.'

Oliver helped Lucille out of her snow jacket, and hung up her jacket, snow trousers, hat and scarf. Then she handed him a bottle of red.

Oliver took it from her with exaggerated graciousness and holding it back, looked at the label.

'Mmm. Shiraz. One of my favourite vineyards. This will go perfectly with the steak.' He flashed her a "thank you" with his big wide smile.

Flicking the tea towel back over his shoulder and grabbing the wine and spatula in one hand, Oliver took Lucille's hand and enthusiastically led her through to the kitchen.

The layout was just the same as Lucille's lodge. The lodge décor was also very similar, just a few different accent colours in the cushions here and there, and different panoramic pictures on the walls. The kitchen was a bit of a mess. Perhaps the cleaners didn't come here often?

Oliver flipped the chips and started another pan warming for the steak. Next, he opened the bottle of red that Lucille had just brought and poured out a little into glasses, while the open bottle aired.

Handing Lucille a glass of wine, Oliver clinked his glass against hers and said, 'Here's to Christmas company.' He looked happily at her and watched her over the wine glasses.

Lucille repeated his toast and sipped the wine too. From behind them she could hear the steaks starting to sizzle and her tummy made little grumbly noises. Oliver winked at her.

✳ ✳ ✳

By the time they'd got to desert, which was a lovely panna cotta that Oliver had somehow found the time to make, Lucille and Oliver had covered most subjects (except age, politics and past relationships) and they were already on to their second bottle of red.

Oliver suggested they adjourn to the living room. While Oliver tended the fire, Lucille cosied up on the large L-shaped sofa to watch him.

Oliver wandered over to her and sat down. Reaching behind him, he pulled a faux-fur blanket towards him and offered it to her in case she was cold. She declined.

Topping up their glasses of red wine, Oliver said, 'So you told me you wrote poetry? Would you recite a piece for me?'

Lucille knew this was going to come up and she was prepared. Trying not to feel embarrassed she tried out one of her attempts from today, on the proviso that he understood she was just playing with the words, and it wasn't really finished. Lucille continued, 'It's inspired by this retreat really. I just need to recharge and come back to me again.'

With sensitive eyes, Oliver nodded as if he understood completely. He sat quietly as Lucille slowly recited:

'Fire in the snow

burning my heart

I heal and grow

fears depart

cut off my pain

wash me anew

cleanse me again

so I can love you'

The space was warm and silent. Lucille could hear the fire crackling in the wood burner. Oliver looked at her with a mixture of what appeared to be admiration and affection. His eyes were soft. Slowly, he placed his glass down on the coffee table, reached over to take Lucille's glass and placed it next to his, then turning back to her he leant slightly forward over her, ran his hand gently along the side of her face and kissed her softly on her mouth.

Lucille responded in kind. Her logic was screaming at her: "What! Are you nuts? You just met this guy. He might have a girlfriend. He might be a serial killer." Whereas the rest of her body was crying out for him and his body, screaming: "Oh! This feels great. This guy is gorgeous. You are a modern woman. Do what you want! Wow!"

Their kissing became more intense as Oliver pushed her back onto the sofa, whispering, 'Seriously, there is something about you. From when you were first angry at me. I am really, really, attracted to you.'

It was about this time that the wine, the fire and

hunger for Oliver's body got the better of Lucille, and she started ripping his shirt off. By the time his muscly torso was holding her clothed body to him there was no going back. It was inevitable.

* * *

Lucille woke to a slightly sore head and the smell of fresh coffee, as Oliver jumped back into bed beside her.

'Morning, gorgeous!' he said, as he slid his hand over her naked body, under the covers.

Lucille could feel herself responding, and the events of the evening before came flooding back to her, only this time sobriety won out. She pushed his hand back and said, 'No. I can't. I don't know what I was thinking last night. I shouldn't have slept with you. It's my fault. I'm sorry.'

Lucille tried to sit up slightly and pulled the pillows up behind her, while clutching at the covers to try and retain a little modesty. Reaching her slim, toned arm out to the bedside table, she gratefully sipped her coffee. 'Thank you for the coffee by the way.'

Oliver looked completely relaxed as he lay against his pillow smiling at her. Eventually, he said, 'I dare you to deny our chemistry is through the roof.'

Lucille blushed and tried to look away as she took another sip of her coffee.

Oliver reached over to her, removed the coffee

cup from her hand and placed it on the bedside table. He straddled her over the covers and said, 'Tell me you don't want me right now as much as I want you.'

Lucille could barely look at him and his naked torso, just inches from her body. This was crazy. Last night had been crazy. What was she doing? Was this just some kind of holiday fling? Two weeks of Oliver and back to her broken life? Should she just enjoy this for what it was and try not to think about it too much?

Oliver leant down to her ear and whispered, 'Every part of my body wants to touch you.'

Slowly she turned her head and their mouths connected in a deep, passionate kiss.

* * *

Lucille dragged herself out of bed. 'I've got to go. I can't just spend two weeks in bed with you. This is too much. I'm supposed to be healing. I'm supposed to be sorting stuff out.'

Oliver watched her sadly as she got dressed. Eventually, he said, 'Can I see you tonight?'

'No. I don't know. I need to think about this. I shouldn't have slept with you. Lots. It's not a good idea.'

Oliver smiled his big wide smile. 'It was a great idea.'

Lucille shot him an angry look.

Oliver said sadly, 'Well, I still want you. Even if

you don't want me.'

Lucille felt mean. She came over to Oliver's side of the bed and allowed herself to briefly touch his hand. 'I'm in a bad place. I don't want to create a mess or make things more complicated. I don't know what I want.'

Oliver looked into her eyes and entwined his fingers through hers, as he said, 'Whatever you need me to be, I can be that.'

Lucille smiled gratefully and let go of his hand saying, 'Besides, the cleaners will be here soon. I don't want them to gossip.'

'No, they won't. I only have them in twice a week. I don't want to add to their work and I don't need to be pampered. I can take care of myself.'

Lucille wanted to laugh, he lived in permanent chaos, but she didn't want to be rude so she said nothing. Smiling goodbye, she descended the stairs and let herself out.

By the time Lucille got back to her lodge, she found the cleaners had been and the firewood was freshly stacked. Going upstairs she ran a hot shower and stood under the soothing hot water. Internally, she was shouting at herself: "What are you doing? Are you crazy?" The problem was, she'd just experienced the best lovemaking of her life. Ever. And every part of her wanted to rush back up there and do it all again. Experience told her that this was going to end in trouble.

* * *

Lucille didn't call Oliver as he'd asked. He'd sent her some pictures throughout the day of some of the beautiful forest views he'd captured. They were incredible pictures. He really was talented. But she didn't reply. In fact, she spent the whole day trying not to think about him, and therefore not able to do much else.

As evening drew in, Lucille decided to put the hot tub on, open a bottle of champagne and try to bubble all her worries, stress and anxiety away.

Lucille sat in the warm water, sipping her champagne, counting the fairy lights, and trying to *think* about things and sort *stuff* out. But the only thought that she kept coming back was Oliver, specifically his body, touching her.

'Hello!' Oliver said, from the bottom of the decking steps. 'You didn't reply to my messages. Did you see the photos?'

Lucille popped her head over the edge of the bubbling hot tub. 'Why do you want me, Oliver?' she asked.

Oliver shrugged as he walked up the steps to the decking. 'I don't really know.' he replied. 'It's a body thing I guess. Every part of me wants to be touching every part of you. But it's a bit more than that. I don't want to hurt you. I do want to make you happy. I don't really know why. I'm trying not to think about it. Just live in the moment. That's what I do.'

'But I'm older than you.'

'I don't care.'

'I have a completely different life from you. We're not compatible.'

Oliver stood by the hot tub, looking softly down into Lucille's imploring grey eyes, and swallowed. 'I know I lead a crazy life. Always travelling here and there. But I've seen a lot and I've learnt a lot. Don't just see me as some young stud who doesn't know what they're doing.'

'I don't. I didn't mean it like that. But do you know what you're doing?'

'Well, I know exactly what I'm about to do.' With that Oliver started undressing on the decking.

'Oliver!' Lucille hissed. 'Someone will see.'

'One. I don't care. Two. We really need to go for a walk tomorrow, so you can see that the other lodges are quite a distance away. Besides. I can't help it.'

Oliver slipped into the hot water and made his way over to Lucille. She passed him her glass of champagne and he took a sip before handing it back to her to finish the glass and put it on the side. Moving his hands back under the water he ran them over her body and she shivered with anticipation. Their mouths passionately connected, under the light of the stars, surrounded by snow.

* * *

Nearly one week had passed by already. Lucille and Oliver had been on walks and she'd watched him take photos, while she wrote poetry in her little notebook. She'd almost half-filled her notebook with words and musings; crossed outlines and re-worked sentences. All these years she hadn't written a thing. She'd thought she'd forgotten how. Her poetry probably wasn't very good, but it was the practising that made it better, like toning a muscle. Oliver said it was great, but he would, Lucille was rose tinted everything to him.

Lucille and Oliver were inseparable. So, it wasn't even a question that they would spend Christmas Day and New Year's Eve together. Lucille warned him that she was leaving 2 January. Oliver said that was okay, but she got the feeling that it wasn't. Oliver also kept asking her about her life back home: what she did, where she lived, when he might be able to see her again.

Lucille lay in his arms, in his lodge, in front of the fire and told him about her life. 'I'm forty-five. I had my son at seventeen and my daughter at eighteen. Colin, my son, is engaged, and Stacey, my daughter, lives with her girlfriend. My husband and I run a chain of boutiques. Well, we did. Until I found out about his multiple affairs with the shop manageresses who were trying to sleep their way up the ladder. So, I left. Just a few weeks ago. It wasn't a happy marriage for quite a while. Yes, it hurt, but strangely, I now feel free.'

'And then you found me.' Oliver said hopefully.

'No. I shouldn't be jumping from one relationship to the next. I need time for reflection.' Lucille said.

'What? Ten years and then you'll want me? That

doesn't make sense and you know it.' Oliver was annoyed.

Lucille lay in the crook of Oliver's arm, looking at the flames dancing in the wood burner. Finally, she answered, 'You don't make sense to me. I don't know how this has happened.'

'Then how did we end up like this?' Oliver asked and squeezed her body closer to his.

'Because I stopped thinking and let my body take over?' Lucille guessed.

'What actually happened is you smelt me, and somewhere in your animal instincts you read my DNA and you know that I'm the one for you.' Oliver said.

Lucille tried to find a logical argument to push back against what Oliver was saying. The problem was, he was right, on a primal level her body *had* picked him. Lucille's thoughts whirred around and around in her head. She desperately needed to work out why she wanted Oliver so much and she only had a week to do so.

❉ ❉ ❉

Christmas Day was bliss. Oliver brought over to Lucille's lodge a tiny tinsel tree that he'd folded up in his large, travelling rucksack. Together they listened to Christmas songs, ate turkey and danced to music, while sipping large glasses of wine and later, champagne.

In the evening they snuggled up in front of

the fire and talked and cuddled. Eventually they couldn't restrain their bodies anymore. Oliver led Lucille by the hand, up the stairs, to her bedroom, where he undressed her and they tenderly made love.

* * *

New Year's Eve was a repeat of the quiet bliss of Christmas Day, except, Oliver insisted that they see in the New Year under the stars.

Oliver had found a quiet spot not too far from the cabins. The clearing in the trees had a view out over the valley, and they could see the earth magic of the New Year laid out before them. The view was of a huge snow-covered valley surrounded by snow-covered mountains and sprinkled with green pine trees, and swathes of pine forests. The snow glowed white in the light of the moon and the stars. It almost seemed to Lucille that the snow sparkled in the half-light. The breeze lightly touched the trees, and she could hear owls in the distance, calling and hooting to each other.

Snuggled up under a windcheater blanket, and cosy in their multiple layers of ski jackets, trousers and woolly hats, they toasted in the New Year with some champagne. A shooting star zipped across the sky.

Oliver looked down at Lucille and said, 'You have to make a wish.'

Lucille screwed her eyes up tight and wished

hard.

Oliver watched her every movement with tender eyes. Then he screwed up his eyes and said, 'I wish for . . .'

'No!' Lucille said, 'Don't tell me or it won't come true.'

Gratefully, Oliver smiled at Lucille and screwing up his eyes again, he made his secret wish.

* * *

It was the night of 1 January. Their last night together before Lucille left. Oliver was due to leave a few days after her. Lucille and Oliver sat snuggled up on the sofa of her lodge watching the fire. Their favourite place to be.

'You really have the most extraordinary job.' Lucille commented. 'So, people just let you stay in places like this, as long as you promote it? All you have to do is take photos and add them to your accounts? People ask you to stay for free?' and she shook her head in wonder.

Oliver just shrugged, 'Yes. I guess for me it seems normal. It's what I do for a living. Sometimes I'll do collections of my photos. I have published two books of my photographs. I have a great life. It suits me.' Oliver pulled Lucille a little tighter to him as they both sat watching the fire. He asked, 'Why don't you join me?'

'What?' Lucille turned around to look at him.

'Come with me. On my adventures. We can have

a base, wherever you want. But we'd be travelling a lot. Take your notebook or a laptop. Write your poetry. Come with me.' Oliver linked his fingers through hers, and looked down into her beautiful grey eyes, 'I'm serious, Lucille. I mean it. Don't go. Come with me.'

Lucille started to think about her family, her friends, her messed up fractured life, her forthcoming divorce. She should probably sort out that mess before she moved on to something else. Her mind whirried and whirred. What should she do? This was crazy. Was it possible she could live this life?

Oliver looked at her with tenderness in his eyes, 'You know, you make much better decisions when you stop thinking and just go with your gut.'

Oliver leant forward and softly kissed Lucille. His lips were as gentle as the breeze and as delicious as honey. Lucille never wanted it to stop. Pulling back a little from him, with love hazed eyes, she replied, 'Okay then.' And they wrapped their arms around each other in a passionate lover's embrace.

6. SNOW ANGELS

Lena stood shivering by the corner of "Atif's Convenience Shop" alongside a busy road, in a busy suburb, in a busy city. Her light-blue eyes looked up at the menacing grey clouds above her. Den had told her this morning that there would be snow today, and he'd reminded her to take her coat.

Lena pulled the thin windcheater jacket a little closer to her skinny body, the bulges in the "hidden" pockets creating strange looking lumps about her torso. She wasn't any warmer, but the act felt comforting. She cowered back a little further into the corner of the shop front, next to the alley, trying to get out of the way of the busy shoppers and letting her thin blonde hair fall around her face.

Perhaps they were shopping for Christmas presents, perhaps they were shopping for food, perhaps they were shopping for what Lena had to sell. There wasn't exactly a "type", usually it was people she'd met before, but sometimes it was someone she didn't know, someone that knew to look for her.

Lena glanced nervously over at the overactive shop door. A sign lay in wait outside, to trap customers back inside, proclaiming: "Fresh Milk". A cold wave of terror rushed down through her body, and the contents of her empty tummy rushed up to meet it, before she expertly buried the thought, before she was even conscious of it.

Lena looked away.

'Selling?' a guy asked quietly bedside her. She hadn't even noticed him in the crowds. She wasn't bothered. It was just a job, right? She quickly looked him up and down. He was short and stocky, clean, he had a black hoody pulled up over his head and grey jogging bottoms. His trainers were trendy and white.

'Fifty or a hundred?' she asked.

'Hundred, love. But not here. Don't want to be seen.' He nodded around the corner, behind her, to the alley.

A hundred. That would be good. If she could just get a few more customers like him, she could go back to Den's flat and get out of the cold. She hated the alley though. It was always a risk.

'A hundred. But no alley.' she said.

'Sorry, too much of a risk.' He smiled kindly in regret and turned to walk away. He seemed nice.

'Okay. Alley. Let's be quick though.' Lena knew there were cameras around the shop front, but she also knew she could be discrete carrying out these sorts of transactions. She was only doing this for him. Because he clearly didn't know how to do this.

* * *

Twenty minutes later, Lena stumbled out of the alley into the cold December afternoon light. She wiped at the blood on her nose. Her jacket was ripped, her body was ripped, her soul had broken long ago. At least he couldn't take that.

The alley was a dead end, so she had to come out eventually, not that anyone cared, they didn't even look at her, not that they'd looked at her when she'd still had bulges in her pockets. No one noticed. She should have insisted that she'd stayed on the corner. Her fault. Her inexperience. She should have realised by now. She'd got cocky and thought she was streetwise. Wrong again.

Lena felt empty, everything that was within her, and of value physically on her, had gone. She couldn't go back. With nothing. She knew she'd be beaten, or worse. Den was kind, of a sort, sometimes. He'd got her this jacket. Perhaps it would be better to go back, end it all, have done. But somehow, she tried to keep going forward not back. Destination unknown.

There were fewer shoppers now. Lena pulled the ripped jacket around her. She'd cleaned up as best she could. Standing outside a furniture store window (which had closed early) she tentatively tried to study her reflection in the glass, and gently reached up to the newly formed bump on her head. The injury was grazed by brick dust and had little train tracks of sticky blood crisscrossing it. Carefully, she pulled her thin blonde hair over the bump, so that no one would know.

Lena headed for the park. Sometimes, when she needed to reconnect and feel at peace she liked to sit on a bench and watch the children play. It reminded her and took her back, almost as if a kind hand were reaching out through time and reason, connecting with her, and taking her to an alternative world, a place she could have been. Sometimes she wondered if this life was all wrong and she actually was living that life, the other one, and that one day she'd wake up. She just wished she knew how to wake up.

Lena gently guided her tired, bent body down onto the cold wood of the bench and watched them play. Like little kittens they tumbled over the multi-coloured, man-bent steel. Underneath, mats of spongy, unwanted tyres were moulded into springboards, to cushion their growing bodies.

They were so adventurous! Lena watched them with awe and an envy without rancour. How she wished she felt like that again. The excitement of flying down the steepest slide you'd ever seen, climbing higher alone that you'd ever done under the watchful guidance of a parent. Knowing it was your achievement alone. Making friends for life with the child you sat next to in class, pinky promise shaking on it, and meaning it, and it lasting forever.

Lena fondly thought back to her best friend from school. Trisha had always been there for her, perhaps she'd help her now? But Lena was too afraid to show her what she'd become. She wished she had the confidence to feel like she did at nine, when your best friend didn't care if your coat was yellow instead of pink. Whereas, somehow, now, turning up in a ripped man's windcheater did matter. And she couldn't really say why.

Happy screeches and screams wafted in bouncy airwaves over to her. Lena smiled as she let the sound therapy soothe her. Her heart warmed and she forgot to be cold.

'Did you fall over?'

Lena opened her eyes to see a little girl standing in front of her, looking her up and down, without fear or privacy. The little girl stared at her ripped jacket and turned her questioning eyes back to Lena, waiting to get her answer.

Lena smiled, 'Yes. Yes, I did sweetheart. Clumsy me!'

'My mum said you need TCP if you fall over, to put on the cuts, and a plaster. But I don't have a plaster or TCP. I have a sweet. A sweet might make it better?' the little girl said.

Lena smiled again as she said, 'Do you know? I think you are quite right. I think a sweet would make me feel better.'

The little girl nodded in affirmation, as if it was no surprise to her that she knew exactly the right medical solution. Fishing around in her pocket she brought out half a bag of part-eaten "Magical Stars" and passed them all to her. 'Here you go. You can have them all. I knew it would make you better.'

Lena graciously accepted the gift. Despite it being the first thing she'd had to eat since a breakfast of neon-pink jam on toast, she didn't gobble it down, instead she cradled the gift in her hands and continued to smile kindly at the little girl.

In a whirlwind of terror, the little girl's mum descended on them. 'Come away!' she hissed at her daughter, spinning her around and dragging her off, without even looking at Lena.

They were gone.

Lena wasn't offended, if she had little cherubs to protect, she wouldn't let them talk to her either. Besides, dusk was falling and it was likely time for the little girl's tea.

Lena didn't know the time. She guessed about five. Den would be expecting her back. He would be angry. She didn't care though, anymore. Everything she had had been taken, and now she was free. There was nothing left to take. Just her and the wind.

Small flakes of twinkling snow started to fall from the bulging grey clouds; lying low over the damp, muddy playpark. The kids had gone. Soon people she didn't want to be around would be here.

Slowly, Lena lifted her stiff body to standing and willed her joints to hinge and her footsteps to move her forward. She would walk the old railway track, it was well lit, and where it rose to the viaduct she could look out over the city, beyond to the hills, and see the newly fallen snow cleaning the streets and fields alike of dirty mud and smog. Perhaps it would cleanse her too?

Lena reached her red, chapped, bony fingers down into the small plastic packet and removed a tiny chocolate star. As she walked, she let it melt onto her tongue. It was delicious.

❋ ❋ ❋

Lena had walked in the failing light until the light was gone, and the snow had fallen thick and bright in the beams of the streetlights. Like fairy dust, little snowflakes swirled around the lamps and landed softly on the ground.

Lena had made the decision when walking along the old railway track, that she wasn't going back. She wasn't exactly sure where she was going, but now that she'd made the decision that she wasn't going back there, she strangely felt a little lighter and safer. She was free. Just like the snowflakes in the wind. Holding out the palm of her hand she watched snowflakes fall on it. They were so beautiful. Each one was unique.

But they were cold!

She should shelter.

Lena walked back into the city. Rather than walk the slushy shop streets and past the last few pre-occupied shoppers, she turned her attention to the suburbs and let her feet wander where they would.

❋ ❋ ❋

Presently, Lena found herself in a smart suburb. The houses here only shared one wall with their neighbours. Only one other set of people to know all the intimate details of your fights. Imagine that! Lena shook her head with the unreality of it. She knew it was a posh neighbourhood because the houses had fancy fir trees in their gardens, decorated with multicoloured Christmas lights and racing icicle flashes encircling their rooves. With the thick, freshly fallen snow, Lena felt as though she had entered an enchanted wonderland. Perhaps she'd even find a grotto with Santa and his elves. Lena smiled to herself.

Pushing her hands inside her pockets, Lena felt the empty sweet packet. The little stars long gone. Walking up to a dog bin on a corner, Lena removed the packet and carefully placed the rubbish inside. The best that she could do.

Lena wandered a little further on until the gardens became bigger and the lights more impressive. Here the houses stood all alone, on their own little patches of land, back from the road, far away from the everyday people. Some still had their curtains open and inside they looked clean, cosy and warm.

Oh, how Lena wished she could be inside. Lena pulled at her ripped jacket, trying to expel the cold winter air. But she would be an embarrassment inside those posh sitting rooms. Better that she was here on the street, and still got to look in.

Lena's head lightly throbbed. Luckily the cold air

numbed the worst of it. The hood on the wind-cheater also kept her hair from the worst of the snow. Her feet were cold and numb though, her skinny jeans were wet and she could feel the cold creeping up her legs. Just one more street and then, she wasn't sure what, then maybe she'd find a bush or something to cuddle up under to pass the night.

Oh! What a street!

Lena rounded the corner and saw, what she believed to be, possibly the best houses in town. Victorian. Five or six bedrooms at least. Little turrets. Double garages. Wrought iron gates much higher than her. Wow.

Lena forgot the cold, and in awe walked along the fresh snow of the pavement. One, perhaps two sets of prints had gone before her. This was almost unchartered territory. Like she was an explorer discovering this wonderous winter land.

One house had the most enormous fir tree, ten feet high at least, covered in large, white, bulb-style lights and silver baubles. Lena was so surprised. They'd even decorated the *outside* trees. She shook her head at the wonder of it.

Another house had Christmas wreaths on all the doors, windows, and the front gates. Lena knew she was probably on a camera, somewhere, but she didn't care. Reaching her red, shaking hand up to the wreath on the gate, she let her skinny fingers caress the soft sprayed fir and real slices of dried orange. Then holding her fingertips to the end of her nose she could almost imagine the smell of orange; the smell of Christmas.

All too soon, Lena reached the end of the road. It was a cul-de-sac. She didn't want it all to end. She also didn't want to go back. Then she saw it. A small metal sign above her head, half-covered with snow, stating: "Resident's Garden".

Around her the snow was drifting, but she could still make out a little path. Boldly she walked on.

❋ ❋ ❋

The path led around to the back of the houses and house gardens, to where the path split in two. One branch led to the fenced and gated, large resident's garden. Lena assumed this was shared between the homeowners all around. The other path led back down behind the houses, along their back gardens.

Which path should Lena choose?

If she went to the garden, she could perhaps find a tree or bush or something, to shelter under for the night. If she took the path behind the houses, she might just get a glimpse of the private, wonderous insides of these magical homes.

Lena pressed her cold hands into the pockets of the windcheater and little bony buttons pressed back along her cold flesh. Furrowing her brow, Lena pulled out her hands and allowed her numbed fingers to investigate. All along the lining of the jacket were little hard buttons, lined up like tin soldiers. Scrabbling at the inner lining of the pocket, Lena found that there was a small hole.

One of the bags of Den's pills must have burst, Lena thought in wonder, and all the little pills had spilled out along the hem of the jacket. Pulling one out she stood looking at the little white pill in the near darkness.

Lena wasn't going back. Den would never know. Shrugging, she popped the pill in her mouth and turned her feet to the path behind the houses.

The first house had a large, glass, kitchen extension sprawling out into the large garden. Lena held her face to the cold iron bars of the back gate and watched a happy couple busying around the enormous space.

The kitchen floor was of limestone flagstone which extended past the kitchen to an eating area and a sitting area beyond. The kitchen cabinets were a pale-blue colour with brushed chrome handles, all in different, twisted, organic shapes. The countertops looked as if they were of some exotic, white, sparkly stone, not unlike the beautiful white carpet of snow that blanketed the garden. There were modern, hanging, pendant lights made from twisted glass, twinkling their glow onto the counters. A few candles were dotted around, and there were glass vases pouring forth bold flowers: gerberas, sunflowers and peonies. The dining table appeared to be made of reclaimed oak, arranged as a long table with reclaimed oak benches either side, and a discarded bottle of wine sitting on top. The sitting area had a peach-coloured, velvet sofa which perfectly complimented the blues of the kitchen. But the most stunning thing, the thing which took Lena's breath away, was the enormous orange cooking range, that took pride of place in the centre of the kitchen. The happy couple were buzzing around it, as it magnificently sat, beaming its heat into the large modern extension.

Oh, how cosy it would be to stand with a glass of wine in front of that stove. Lena could almost feel the warmth.

Suddenly, the couple left the glass extension and the lights went out. The vision was gone.

With a sigh, Lena pushed her hands into her pockets, searching for warmth and comfort. Instead, she found a little pill. Shrugging, she popped it into her mouth and stumbled on to the next house. Wondering what she might see next.

Lena wasn't disappointed.

Another huge extension pulled out from behind the old Victorian house. Despite the base of the extension being of local limestone, the top was again all glass, and there were glass double doors looking out on to the garden. The curtains hadn't been pulled over the glass doors. Lena could see quite clearly in.

It was a dinner party!

There were ladies dressed in champagne-coloured, sparkly dresses and rich, dark-coloured, velvet jumpsuits. They swayed and laughed beside men wearing pastel-coloured shirts and cashmere, V-neck jumpers. The table took up at least half the extension space and there must have been more than a dozen guests.

Lena watched as a proud-looking man stood up brandishing a carving knife and fork, and his beaming husband held aloft the turkey fresh from the kitchen. The guests cheered and clapped in appreciation; some even raised their glasses. It looked magical. Oh, how Lena wished she could taste a little of the turkey. She could almost imagine it in her mouth.

Then, the guest nearest the glass double doors, got up and closed the curtains. The vision was gone.

Lena stood in the cold and the dark. The smell of cooked turkey still lingering in her nostrils. Reaching inside the pocket of her jacket, she pulled out another pill and ate it. She moved on.

The next house also had a large extension. Again, this extension was a mixture of limestone and glass. But there were no people inside, in fact it was almost entirely dark, except for a Christmas tree. A grand, thick, silver fir. It was adorned with frosted, pastel-coloured, round, fairy lights and pink, green and yellow ribbons. The baubles were all glass, but some had silver gemstones or faux pearls glued on. The baubles twinkled in the light of the fairy lights. It was quite possibly the most beautifully decorated, gloriously pretty tree, Lena thought she'd ever seen.

A real tree. Lena could remember quite clearly the last time she'd had a real Christmas tree. She shook the thought away, but still it came up. She tried all the tricks she could think of, but this thought persisted.

* * *

Lena sat with three children around a Christmas tree.

'Mummy, are you sure Santa will come this year?'

'I can promise you my darling, he is coming.' Lena replied.

Another little voice: 'But Mummy, he didn't come last year.'

'Oh, my lovely, I think he just got lost. I promise you,' reaching out, Lena stroked the cheek of her young daughter's face, 'I made sure he knows where we live now. I promise you he will come because you are all such good little children.' her daughter smiled back at her. 'Now off to bed. He won't come if you're not sleeping!' . . .

Lena stood in front of the fridge, holding the empty milk bottle. The children were safely snug in their beds. She would just pop next door to borrow some milk for their breakfast. She'd been so busy with the presents that she'd quite forgotten to get the milk . . .

Lena's eyes were wide with terror and her mouth made the shape of someone screaming, but there was no sound, just the vision: Lena, crazed, desperate, clawing over the policewomen with the kind brown eyes, desperate to race into the inferno of her home. In the window, the Christmas tree stood engulfed in a mass of flames. Smoke and flames gushed from every window. The heat was overwhelming. Lena had stayed away too long.

Gone.

Lena stood in the dark air and the soft, sparkling snow, her head pressed against the cold iron of the gate, her forehead thumping like a little separate heartbeat, in front of her the most impossibly beautiful Christmas tree she'd ever seen. Lena craned forward, pushing against the gate. The gate gave way a little and creaked quietly in the late of the evening.

Lena looked around at the empty alley behind her. No one was there. Perhaps there were cameras. She didn't know. She didn't care. Carefully, Lena stepped forward onto the untouched snow, into the garden, and walked over to the extension.

Despite the darkness beyond, the beautiful twinkling of the Christmas lights illuminated the presents under the tree. Lena could see three, red, felt stockings, attached to the thick oak mantelpiece which ran over the top of the modern fireplace, housing an unlit wood burner. Lena could almost picture her children here: their excitement putting up the stockings, checking with her for reassurances that Santa would come, whizzing in circles and shaking presents under the tree. Too excited to go to bed. Not wanting to sleep.

The timer on the tree lights clicked off and the extension was plunged into darkness.

Lena held on to the windowsill and tried to peer into the darkness. Willing the vision to come back, but it didn't.

The snow was cold and her jeans were wet through. Lena's feet and hands were cold and aching. Still, she willed the vision to return, but reality wouldn't let it.

Lena pushed her hands further into the pockets of the windcheater. Little pills pushed back at her sore fingers. Carefully, one by one she pulled them out and lined them up along her left hand. Twelve pills in total. What did she care? She wasn't going back. Den would never know. Opening her mouth wide, Lena threw them in, crunching down with purpose and swallowing. She tried to imagine that they tasted like turkey. Scooping a little snow from the window ledge, she ate some of that too and swallowed heavily.

Looking around the dark of the garden, the blanket of soft, sparkling snow called to Lena. It was untouched and beautiful, it looked so comfy.

Stepping into the middle of the garden, Lena lay down and looked up at the sky above her. The snow had stopped and the clouds had cleared. She almost believed that through the lights of the city she could see a few stars poking through. She almost thought she saw a shooting star.

The snow was sheltering and soft. Lena felt her tired, broken body relax. She let her eyes close and the cool air soothe her fears away.

'Mummy!' came the voice. 'Mummy. Is it wake up

time? Did Santa come?'

Lena opened her eyes to see her daughter, Libby. Libby was just the spit of her, with the same thin blonde hair and bony hands, and the same light-blue eyes. She was urgently tugging at the ripped windcheater.

Beside her daughter stood her two boys, Benjie and Jaxon. Jaxon was only three, still only three, and held his brother's hand tightly. Benjie said, 'Mummy, Granny said we had to wake you up because it's Christmas. You need to come with us. We want to go and check our stockings.'

There was a part of Lena's mind that reasoned this wasn't logical. She was in a garden, lying in the snow. She was cold. But that part of logic didn't seem the most real. What was real were her three beautiful children, standing in front of her, asking her to come with them.

Reality won.

'But how can I come my darling?' Lena asked.

Jaxon answered, 'Mummy, you fly!'

'Fly?'

Libby explained, 'Snow angels, Mummy. Do you remember when we made snow angels? We need to do it like that.'

Lena smiled at her daughter. She did remember when they went sledging and made snow angels.

Benjie lay down in the snow with Jaxon and said, 'Come on, Mummy, I'll show you how.' and started swishing his legs and arms around in the snow. Jaxon was laughing and followed suit.

Libby lay down the other side of Lena and said, 'Come on, Mummy, you're not trying.'

Lena's arms and legs were like lead. She was encased in a cold tomb of snow. She couldn't move.

Libby looked over to her mum in desperation. 'Mummy, you have to try.'

'I am trying, darling. It's hard. My legs and arms are cold.'

Libby replied, 'But it is lovely and warm when we get there. Please try, Mummy.'

With herculean effort, with every last gasp of energy in her thin, bony body, Lena tried to move her arms and legs. The effect was small at first, but as she got into the rhythm, she was able to move her legs and arms further and further. *Swish*, *swish*, *swish* in the snow.

'That's it Mummy,' said Benjie, 'We're flying.'

* * *

'Dad! Dad! There's a snow angel in the garden.'

Pete opened his bleary eyes to find his daughter tugging at his pyjamas, trying to drag him out of bed.

'Dad. There's a snow angel in the garden.' she said again urgently.

Pete wiped his hand over his forehead and allowed himself to be dragged over to the window, to where his son had ripped back the curtain, and was looking down at the garden with a strange look on his face. Pete's youngest daughter clamoured at her father's leg, wanting to be carried, knowing something different had happened and wanting the security of being safe with her dad.

Pete looked down at the back garden. There, in the middle of the snow-covered lawn, was, what looked like, the body of a person. They were surrounded by funny marks in the snow. The back gate was open.

'See.' his daughter said. 'See, snow angels. We've had snow angels in our garden.'

There were indeed three sets of snow angel markings in the snow. But the fourth one contained a shape of what looked like a person. Pete swore.

'Stay here.' Pete commanded. Then he turned to his son and said, 'Michael, call the police. And an ambulance.' Grabbing his dressing gown, Pete rushed downstairs, pushed his feet into his boots, unlocked the back door, and rushed into the back garden.

The pale blue-white woman was clearly quite dead. No need for an ambulance then. The back gate was open but the house hadn't been broken into.

Pete felt for a pulse, and from the frozen clasped hand fell some small white pills.

'Drugs.' Pete said, almost to himself, and grimaced. He couldn't feel a pulse, her hands were stiff, the body was deathly cold. To be sure, Pete gently lifted her eyelid, just under, what looked like, a very nasty head injury. She had a beautiful light-blue eye with an unfocussed, enlarged, black pupil. Her eyes were the same blue colour as his late wife's eyes. He closed her eyelid. Quite dead.

Behind him, Pete could hear his son ushering someone through the house towards him. It was the police. A female officer with kind brown eyes, stepped forward to assess the dead young woman.

'I don't know her.' Pete explained. 'I don't know who this woman is.' he said in his defence.

The female officer bent over the body and held the palm of her hand to the side of the young woman's face as she gently said, 'No. It's okay, sir. I don't think you would know her. But I think I do.' Turning back to the young lady, she slowly leant forward and kissed her cold, bruised forehead goodbye.

7. FLY AWAY WITH ME (ON MY SLEIGH)

Jim stood in front of the check-in desk at Edinburgh airport, trying to take in what the lady behind the desk was saying. She was about five-foot-seven, with blonde hair neatly twisted up in a bun and green-hazel eyes. She had a prominent nose and a soft, long face. She had just the right amount of curve to her body. She seemed nice so he didn't want to be cross. But clearly there was some mistake.

Jim leant forward and looked at her name badge. 'Carly,' he said in his deep, resonant voice and Scottish accent, 'clearly there has been some mistake, I'm meeting my friends here for a stag do, in Dublin this weekend. Could you check again?'

Carly looked at the tall (at least six feet) man in front of her. He was good looking in slim "Captain America" sort of way. He had lovely blue eyes, a long face with laughter lines, and brown hair which was trimmed quite short over the back and sides. His arms were thick and muscly and he had slim, muscly legs. He was wearing jeans and a fitted check shirt. She watched him run his hand over his face in stress.

Carly had had a few difficult customers today, but she could sympathise with this man. He seemed nice. Smiling kindly, she said, 'Mr. Angus, I do understand your frustration, but this ticket is booked for the seventeen forty-five flight to Dublin for Thursday 17 December. Today is the 16 December. You are one day early.'

Carly could see that the queue behind the man wasn't too long, and her colleague beside her was also checking passengers in for the seventeen forty-five flight. She could give him a little help and time, besides the man looked stressed and disappointed.

Carly tried to help him further, 'Do you have the name of one of your fellow passengers?'

'Fraser McLean.' Jim promptly replied.

Carly typed the details into her computer and checked the flights for 17 December. Looking up at Jim, she said, 'Mr. Fraser McLean has a seat on tomorrow's flight. I'm sorry. There are seats on today's flight, so you can take the flight today, or stay on tomorrow's flight with the rest of the party?'

Jim knew he needed to make a quick decision. He didn't have accommodation in Dublin for tonight as they'd booked a shared flat and clearly that wouldn't be ready until tomorrow now. He also wanted to be with the crowd and to share the excitement of the flight over. The trouble was he'd travelled nearly four hours to get here today, so he certainly didn't want to repeat that journey. He'd just have to find accommodation for tonight in Edinburgh and meet with the guys tomorrow.

Smiling gratefully, Jim said, 'I'm an idiot. Can you keep me on the flight tomorrow? Thursday 17 December. Thank you. Can you check me in now?'

Carly met his eyes and smiled back. 'Yes. I can check you in now, sir. You can drop your bags off tomorrow before the flight.' She stared typing in his details: Mr. James Angus. She smiled at his passport photo. He seemed nice.

'Please, call me Jim.' Jim said.

Carly flicked her eyes up at him. Their eyes connected. Carly flushed slightly and dropped her eyes back at the computer screen, schooling herself, "Keep professional, Carly. He's just a passenger passing through. Do your job."

Smiling and printing off Jim's details, Carly handed them to him and said, 'You are checked in for the seventeen forty-five flight, Thursday 17 December. Please leave at least an hour to drop off your bags before your flight.'

Jim smiled back at her and gratefully took his documents. 'Thanks, Carly.' he said.

Carly's heart did a little flutter.

* * *

Carly had had a long day. Her feet were tired from standing in heels all day. She was looking forward to going home and having a hot shower and something to eat. It was nearly eight in the evening and most of the passengers had left for their destinations now.

Some of Carly's colleagues were still busy. Some travellers were wandering around looking lost. The airport never really slept; it just got a bit quieter overnight. Carly had Sunday and Monday off. Not so far away. Perhaps she'd do some last-minute Christmas shopping.

Carly's mind busied with thoughts of this and that. Planning, organising, lists, work stress. She slipped on her coat, tied the belt, grabbed her navy suede gloves and neat leather handbag, and started to make her way through the airport to the car park and her car, to go home.

As Carly passed by "Ye Olde Pub" in the middle of the terminal, she was surprised to see Jim, sat at one of the high tables, a half-drunk lager in front of him. He was reading a book. Just as she was about to walk on, he looked up from his book, caught her eye, smiled and shrugged.

Smiling in reply, Carly wandered over.

'Hi again!' Jim said.

'Hi. You didn't stay in town?' Carly asked.

Jim gave an exaggerated exhale and raised his eyebrows good humouredly. 'Apparently there is a climate conference on. After about an hour I gave up trying to find a room. I'll just kip on some of the seats tonight and go into Edinburgh tomorrow to use up some time before the flight.'

'Oh no. You're not having much luck with your journey.' she sympathised.

Bravely, Jim said, 'I always seem to be a bit luckier around you.' and nervously laughed.

Carly smiled, blushed and looked at her feet.

'Hey,' Jim continued, 'I was just about to have some dinner. Do you want to join me? As a thank you for helping me out today.'

Carly couldn't help herself, despite being tired, she absolutely did want to have dinner with him.

'Thank you, yes. Although, I didn't do so much you know.' Carly replied.

Jim smiled, packed up his book and put his phone back in his pocket, collected his rucksack and lager, and directed them to a quiet corner of the "pub".

* * *

Carly and Jim got on brilliantly. Carly forgot to be tired and Jim forgot to be bored. They covered all sorts of subjects: Jim's job (he was an engineer), siblings, where Jim and Carly lived, where they came from, schools, universities. Jim was most impressed to find that Carly spoke two foreign languages: Spanish and German. They enjoyed a meal of fish and chips and talked until the staff at the pub chucked them out. Jim even suggested they get a coffee, but it was getting late and Carly had to work tomorrow, so reluctantly she declined.

'So, you're working here again tomorrow?' Jim said.

'Yes, my next day off is Sunday.' Carly replied.

'Perhaps I could meet you for lunch tomorrow

then, if you're around?' Jim ventured.

Carly smiled shyly. 'Okay. That would be nice.' she said.

Carly and Jim smiled at each other and Carly's heart made tiny backflips.

❉ ❉ ❉

Jim kept his word and took Carly to lunch the next day. She only had fifty minutes, so the conversation was a little more direct.

'I'm guessing you don't have a boyfriend then? As you're having lunch with me.' Jim asked.

Carly blushed. 'I don't have a boyfriend. I've actually had a fairly awful time with guys. Lots of disastrous relationships.'

Jim pulled his eyebrows together in concern, 'But you're gorgeous!' Then stopped and smiled. He'd said too much, but bravely ploughed on. 'I mean. I can't understand why a guy wouldn't treat you like a princess.'

Carly looked sad, 'I just seem to attract guys that seem nice and turn out to be mean. Mean to me that is.' She sighed. 'I just don't have much luck with guys, that's all.'

Jim tried to cheer her up, 'I think that's their fault if they don't appreciate you, not yours. Hey, just for the record I think you're great.'

Carly blushed at the compliment. 'Thank you.' she said. Then mustering her courage, she asked, 'So, what about you? Why are you single?'

Jim sighed and summed it up with, 'Always the bridesmaid, never the bride.' He set his mouth to an upside-down smile. 'It'll be great to be with the guys this weekend, but I'm the only one in the group who's still single. Everyone in my friendship group from university is happily settled too. It just hasn't seemed to work out that way for me.'

Carly tried to cheer him up. 'Hey. It's better to be single than with the wrong person.'

Jim shrugged his shoulders as he said, 'Yeah. I know it. Just living it can be a little lonely sometimes.' He tried to lighten the mood. 'Do you want some pudding?' he asked.

Spying the clock at the corner of the eatery, Carly said, 'I'm so sorry, I can't. I've got to get back. Thank you so much for lunch, and dinner last night. You didn't have to. Do you want me to split the bill?'

'Not at all. It is my pleasure.' Jim replied, standing up with her. He gulped heavily and said, 'Perhaps, and it's perfectly okay to say no, would you be okay if I took your number?'

Carly smiled and gave it to him. Then nodding their goodbyes and joking that they might see each other later, Carly left.

* * *

Jim certainly did see Carly later. This time he was surrounded by a group of noisy, boisterous guys. As the group queued for the check-in desks and bag drop, Jim made sure that his bag was checked in by Carly, even though the guys teased him about it.

'Hello again!' Carly said smiling.

'Hey.' Jim said winking, as he passed her his passport and boarding pass that she'd printed for him yesterday. Behind him the guys cheered.

Carly blushed and felt quite self-conscious. Jim had clearly said something to them about taking her to dinner and lunch. With so much testosterone around, Carly started to feel a little intimidated. As she tapped Jim's details into the computer and moved his rucksack along the conveyor belt, she tried to focus on doing her job efficiently. All the while she was aware of Jim looking at her. Intently.

Glancing up at Jim, Carly smiled and passed him back his passport and boarding pass with his baggage sticker attached. 'Have a lovely flight and time in Dublin.' she said.

'As long as it's as nice as the day I've just had, then it will be great.' Jim looked intently at her.

Carly smiled and Jim moved to the side so that she and her colleague could continue checking in the high-spirited group of men.

When the queue had gone and Carly had time for some reflection, she felt a little sad. That was it then. Jim would be returning Sunday and she was off on Sunday. Perhaps he'd call her, but he was off to have fun with the guys, by the time Sunday came around she'd be no more than fleeting memory. Something that could have been.

Carly's colleague, Debbie, leant over to her from behind the check-in desks and said in a loud whisper. 'The guy in the checked shirt was a complete hunk, and he was checking you out, did you see?'

Carly shook her head sadly and said, 'I've got a story for you. Do you want a cup of tea?'

'Excellent idea!' Debbie replied.

Both ladies placed the closed signs on the desks and made their way around the back to the tearoom.

* * *

'Well.' Debbie said, clutching her still warm, empty teacup and helping herself to another custard cream from the tin. 'He seems a little better than the normal oglers, and he bought you dinner, twice. I like him.'

Carly waved her phone at her friend. The screen was blank. 'Except he's taken my number and no messages yet.'

Debbie proclaimed, 'Have you really shown him you're interested? Perhaps you need to "bump" into him sometime. Then he'll remember how lovely you are.'

'I can't stalk him.' Carly replied, horrified.

'No, but you know when his flight back is. How many airmiles have you got? Plus, Sunday's late flight still has seats and you've got the day off. You could take the morning flight to Dublin, do some shopping and happen to take the same flight back. That's not stalking, that's coincidence.'

Carly pursed her lips together. 'Don't suppose you're free Sunday?' she asked.

'Nope, family lunch.' Debbie rolled her eyes in anticipation of it. 'Besides he doesn't want two women, he just wants one.'

Carly retorted, 'A stag do in Dublin? I expect he'll be getting an eyeful of lots of women all weekend.'

'Yeah, but I bet he doesn't ask them to dinner.' Carly sighed as Debbie continued, 'Just think about it okay? You have the airmiles burning a hole in your pocket. It's just a thought.'

✻ ✻ ✻

Carly stood in front of the bookstand at the end of the terminal waiting for her flight Sunday morning. Part of her felt silly and part of her felt excited. Was she mad to be doing this? Debbie had suggested it so it must be all right? The problem was that her relationships always ended badly. Part of her didn't want the pain again, and part of her was ever hopeful that true love and romance existed. That love was still waiting for her, around that ever-elusive corner.

Carly ran her eyes over the bookshelf as a title caught her eye: *Single Women – get the guy!* Intrigued, Carly picked it up and read the overview on the back:

Always the bridesmaid never the bride? Alice Evans is one of the UK's top dating experts, and, using a mixture of psychology, biology and her extensive dating knowledge as an Agony Aunt for the Daily Prophet, she outlines her five-step program for attracting the right man and navigating the early stages of a relationship. Reviewers call this book . . .

Funny how fate has a way of leaving breadcrumbs along the trail to the right path. Clutching the book, Carly felt this was the perfect book to accompany her on her adventure.

Paying for her purchase, Carly heard the boarding call for her gate, and rushed to join the queue of passengers to Dublin.

It was cold outside on the tarmac at Edinburgh airport. Carly didn't have much luggage, just a large bucket bag. Being airport staff, she'd been moved to a spare seat at the front of the plane before the dividing curtains; demarking first class. So, while the other passengers struggled onboard with their bags, past her down the narrow aisle, Carly wiggled her bottom in her seat, got comfy and opened the first page of her book.

Carly was engrossed. It was somewhere over the Irish Sea that she read the haunting words of chapter three: "Don't Chase. Men Hunt." Carly furrowed her eyebrows and shifted uncomfortably on her seat as she craned her head in closer to the text.

The biggest mistake the modern woman makes is chasing a man. Ladies, I'm telling you: "No!" don't do this. Men need to hunt. If you chase, then he has you without effort and you have diminished your value. Men need to feel they've won. "What if he doesn't chase you?" you may ask. Sadly, ladies, if he doesn't chase then he doesn't value you, and was merely flirting. Pick up your precious heart and move on. The intensity of the hunt tells you about his feelings for you. The longer the hunt, the more he is able to develop feelings for you. This is your warning: Do not chase men. Let men hunt you.

Carly reread the chapter several times to be sure she really understood what the author was trying to tell her. In essence, Carly was supposed to, what, sit and do nothing? And if she was on his flight back from Dublin then she was, *easy*? Jim wouldn't value her. She'd be putting herself on the discard pile.

A cold shiver went up Carly's back. She needed to get off this flight! Carly looked out of the window onto the grey Irish Sea below her. She needed to book a different flight back. As soon as she landed, she'd go to the check-in desk and get the next flight back to Edinburgh.

Holding tightly to the closed book, Carly thanked her lucky stars that she'd read this in time. Finding this book was a stroke of good luck. She could have spoilt everything. That is if anything was ever destined to happen.

* * *

Carly looked at Michelle. She was always on the phone to Michelle; they'd been on some of the same training schools together.

'Could you check again?' Carly pleaded.

Michelle moved aside for Carly to see her screen as she said, 'I'm sorry, it's overbooked. I think it is due to people travelling back for Christmas and needing ongoing transport the other end. Some of the ones that don't make this flight will probably be on your twenty thirty-seven flight this evening. I'm sorry Carly. There's nothing I can do.'

Carly sighed inwardly and resigned herself to the fact that she was really making a complete mess of this. She wished she'd never come. She wished she'd read the book before talking to Debbie. But it wasn't Debbie's fault, it was hers. Messed up, upside-down relationships. Carly's New Year's resolution would be to get a relationship counsellor and sort this all out.

'It's okay Michelle. It's not your fault.' Carly said. 'I'll get the twenty thirty-seven flight as booked.'

'Are you off into Dublin?' Michelle asked.

'I've kind of lost the heart for it now. I think I'll stay here and read my book.' Carly replied.

'Don't suppose you fancy catching up for lunch and a chat?' Michelle said.

'Do you know, that would be nice.' Carly replied. She was glad of her friends.

* * *

Carly had enjoyed her lunch with Michelle. Over lunch she'd spilled the beans as to why she was here, and that, although it had been Debbie's idea, she'd gone with it but changed her mind. Carly brought out the book and showed Michelle.

Michelle read the back of the book, looked at Carly thoughtfully and placing her hand on her arm, told her not to worry.

After lunch, Carly found a nice quiet corner and spent the rest of the afternoon eating chocolate croissants, drinking café lattes and reading her book. She'd reached the final chapter when she heard the call for her flight back to Edinburgh. "What a fruitless day!" She thought to herself. Now her only job was to make sure that Jim didn't see her on the flight home.

Skirting around the crew at the gate, Carly was aware of a group of boisterous, tired, noisy men near one of the confectionary dispensers. Carly tried to not look as she talked to some of her colleagues and left the gate to board the flight before the other passengers.

Once again, Carly was in first class, distinguished by the curtain dividing the first three rows of the plane. When she boarded the plane, she wrapped herself up in a blanket, turned her head towards the dark window, and hoped to goodness Jim didn't recognise her.

Carly heard the other passengers starting to board, and resolutely kept her head turned towards the window. On and on they came. To try and distract herself, Carly pulled out the book and huddled up to the window waiting for the flight to depart. From the front of the plane, she could hear:

'But there must be some mistake. I'm in first class.' said a man's angry voice.

'I'm sorry sir, but this ticket clearly places you in seat seventeen-D, you will need to move on down the aisle.' replied the calm voice of the steward.

'But I paid for this!' the angry man said again.

'I appreciate that, sir, however, the flight is very full. You can return to the gate or you can take this flight. The seat you have been allocated is seventeen-D. I will warn you the next flight to Edinburgh is tomorrow morning.' said the steward.

'But I checked. I checked my tickets. I was allocated seat two-B. I don't see when this mix up could have happened. Let me tell you that as soon as I arrive in Edinburgh, I will be making a complaint to the airline.' said the angry man.

'Absolutely, sir. I perfectly understand. If you would be so kind as to take your seat, other passengers are boarding.' the steward replied.

Behind the angry man, Carly could hear a noisy group of men stomping up the steps. She shrunk under her blanket a little further and intently stared at her book.

One by one the noisy men filed passed Carly and proceeded to fill up the seats around seventeen-D.

'Hello.' a familiar voice said beside her.

Fearfully, Carly popped her head up from her book and met the kind blue eyes of Jim. Carly flushed bright red.

Jim continued, 'I'm sorry. It seems there has been a mix up with the seats. I think I've got the seat next to you.'

Carly looked up in horror at the seat name, "two-B".

'Oh, of course.' Carly replied, sitting up straight, and trying to keep her composure.

'I didn't expect to see you on my flight.' Jim said.

Carly flushed harder. 'There were some spare seats and I decided to do a little Christmas shopping as Dublin is so lovely.' Trying to cover her tracks she said, 'It's a perk of the job. We take flights all the time.' she said.

'Oh yes. I bet. I never really thought about that. So, what did you buy?' Jim asked.

'Err, books mainly. For the family.' Carly hastily and surreptitiously stowed her book *Single Women – get the guy!* into her bag and kicked the bag under the seat in front of her.

'Oh nice.' Jim furrowed his brow, thinking Dublin was quite a long way to buy some books. Forging on, he said, 'I'm sorry I didn't text or anything. It's been a busy weekend.'

Carly smiled politely. 'No. Not at all. I hope you had fun.'

'Yeah!' Jim replied, 'It's been wild.'

From somewhere back in the cabin, Carly could hear some men chanting some sort of stag do song. Almost as if it were a ritual rite of passage. The aircrew at the front of the plane started making their initial checks and reviewing the passenger on board list.

From behind Carly and Jim, one of Jim's friends came up the aisle and said, 'Hey mate. I think there's been a mix up in the seats. There's a guy with us and he said you've got his seat.'

Jim looked up and said, 'Oh really?'

'Yeah, mate. He's getting a bit grumpy. I said you'd be okay to move.'

Jim thought about it and said, 'Nope. Pretty sure this is the right seat.'

Jim's friend looked at him strangely, then looked over at Carly, his eyebrows raising with recognition, he then looked back to Jim, and said, smiling, 'No problems mate. Just thought I'd check.' Jim and the friend exchanged a nod as the friend retreated back down the aisle.

Jim looked sideways at Carly and said, 'Seems there have been lots of muddle ups over the seats.' He raised his eyebrows.

Carly was mortified and blushed harder. 'Err. Yes.' Inside all she could think was: Michelle! She'd need to have a serious word with her and Debbie when she was in work Tuesday. For now, she just had to navigate sitting next to this gorgeous guy and not chase him. How on earth was she to show she was interested by not being interested. This was a pickle. Carly decided to say nothing at all.

Jim shut off his phone. The plane taxied along the runway and took off. Still, Carly said nothing. Jim took out his book.

The confectionary trolly came around. Leaning over, Sarah, the air stewardess said to Carly, 'On the house.' and passed her two half-bottles of champagne and two plastic flutes.

Jim gratefully received his orange juice from the air stewardess, then turning to Carly, as Sarah departed, he said, 'Blimey, you really do get some perks.' He started laughing.

Carly looked embarrassed. She said, 'I don't think I could manage two. Would you like one?'

'Well considering my liver has had a bit of a workout this weekend. Why not?' Jim replied.

Jim opened the champagne for them and poured it out into the flutes. He proposed a toast saying, "Wasn't it lucky they'd met on the flight?" And as the bubbles met their bloodstreams, Carly relaxed and they spent the rest of the flight chatting.

By the time Carly and Jim reached the airport in Edinburgh, it was almost as if it were Thursday all over again. Carly and Jim disembarked first.

As Jim waited for his friends to alight, he said, 'Hey, it really has been great getting to know you. I have your number. I promise, I will definitely text.'

'Thank you. I look forward to it. That would be nice.' Carly replied with a smile.

Boldly, perhaps it was the champagne they'd consumed at altitude, Jim leant forward and kissed Carly on the cheek. 'See you around, eh?' he said.

Carly smiled and said, 'Yes, see you around.' Her heart felt like fluttering tissue paper in the breeze, but with the words of Alice Evans's advice still burning into her eyes, she knew she needed to exit, and quickly. Carly needed to leave him wanting more.

Smiling up at Jim and mentally saying "goodbye" (because there was always a chance that he was flirting and that this wasn't a hunt for him), Carly prepared herself to never see Jim again, as she turned around and calmly made her way out of the airport to the car park and her car.

* * *

Carly was busy over the next week. Reuniting passengers with loved ones and trying to get them home. She had lunch with her mum on Christmas Day. Boxing Day she was back in at work to mop up the debris of missed and delayed flights over Christmas.

Carly's phone remained empty. No texts, no calls from Jim.

Carly sighed. Well. As Alice Evans said: better to know it was just flirting and move on gracefully, than to chase and be treated poorly. In all of Carly's relationships, she had been treated poorly, and she didn't want the heartache of that again.

But, Jim had seemed so nice.

Carly sighed again. That's just the way it was. She had to accept it.

* * *

It was Wednesday 30 December. Debbie was in work. Carly had already talked about the Dublin trip and found that Debbie and Michelle had been in cahoots to make sure it worked out for Carly. They were equally disappointed that Jim hadn't texted or called. Carly had even shown Debbie the book. But Debbie dismissed it as codswallop and said that when men fall in love they just know.

But Jim hadn't fallen in love, had he? He hadn't even sent Carly a "Happy Christmas" text.

Carly started checking in the first passengers of the day. Debbie next to her was like a can of Mexican jumping beans. It was even worse when Laura, on Carly's opposite shift, turned up. Apparently, there'd been a mix up of rotas. Laura hung around and offered to help out now that she was in, but Carly insisted she rest up, particularly as she was four months pregnant.

Tapping away at the computer on the check-in counter, Carly was most surprised to see, further down the queue, Jim, with his puffer jacket under his arm, his check shirt stretched across his muscly chest and a big grin. He was looking back at her.

Carly tried to remain professional and continued to check in passengers. When Jim's turn came in the queue, he insisted on waiting for Carly rather than Debbie.

Standing in front of Carly's desk, Jim said, 'Check-in for two please.'

Carly looked puzzled and leant around to look behind him. 'Err. Do you have their passport?' she said.

'I think all you need is a driving licence.' He pushed the flight details and his passport over the counter towards her. It was a return flight to London for today, for himself and Carly.

Carly looked at the documents and pulled her eyebrows together. This was all very strange. Behind her, she could hear Laura back from the tea-room.

From behind Carly, Laura said, 'Ah, Mr. Angus. So good to speak to you on the phone. I assume the ticket details are correct?'

Jim replied, 'Yes, all correct, many thanks to yourself and Debbie.'

From the corner of her eye, Carly could see a little half-smile on Debbie's face as she checked in the next passenger. Carly looked around to Laura confused, as Laura gently moved Carly out from her seat, logged her off the system, logged herself in, and proceeded to check in Carly and Jim for the next flight to London.

Handing Jim their boarding passes, Laura said, 'Boarding is in fifty minutes, departure gate five.'

Carly stood open mouthed as Jim turned to Carly and said, 'Fly away with me?'

Blushing, Carly replied, 'Yes.'

8. ENCHANTED ESCAPE

Joe had moved to the little alpine chalet with his parents when he was eight. From the moment he joined school, he and Louis were inseparable.

Joe loved going to school, not that he was particularly bothered by learning and schooling, but because he got to spend all day in the presence of his best friend; the one person who understood him and made time for him above all others. Intelligent, exuberant, Louis.

As Joe and Louis grew older their friendship stood firm. Joe was the stable one, mild-mannered, careful, diligent, measured. He had brown hair, brown eyes and a non-descript, average face that matched his personality. Louis had white-blonde hair, piercing blue eyes, sharp features and all the crazy ideas. Like making go-carts and racing them down the hill in the village as fast as they could; or going up into the hills and creating dens and secret hideaways, camouflaged with tree branches.

Joe and Louis lived for their time together and it was always fun. Both Joe and Louis's parents commented on their inseparable bond, shook their heads, and wondered how two such different people never grew tired of each other. But Joe and

Louis's friendship stood firm. More than that, their compounded memories and shared experiences bound them together through the passage of time. In the chaos of the world, the duo knew they could always depend on the other, and even if no one else believed them, they would always believe in each other.

That was why, despite all reason, when Louis came back from the woods one day and said he'd seen fairies, Joe didn't tell him that such things didn't scientifically exist, or to stop making up stories. Rather, they sat together quietly on the swing seat at the end of Louis's parent's balcony, overlooking the summer valley below, while Joe listened and Louis explained.

'I went up into the woods to pick wild strawberries for Mum.' Louis explained. 'I'd found a new a secret spot, a little clearing, it's quite high up. I don't think many people go there.'

Joe nodded, listening intently to his friend, 'Is it far to walk?' Joe asked.

'Not too far. I think we should go. I want to show you.' Louis said.

'You don't think it was a fleeting thing, and that the fairies will move on?' asked Joe.

'No. The trees all around the clearing were different too, with funny twists and holes. I think it might be a fairy settlement. Where they live. I don't know why I didn't see it before.' said Louis.

'Perhaps it's enchanted. Perhaps they wanted you to see it.' reasoned Joe.

The friends exchanged glances and Louis looked at his feet. Louis asked, 'But why now? Why do they want to show me this now?'

Louis raised his eyes to the concerned eyes of his friend. Joe replied, 'I don't know Louis. But I agree, I do think we should go back and check it out again together.'

Louis nodded, relieved. Joe was practical and sensible. Joe would sort it all out. Perhaps he'd had too much sun, or not enough water to drink? Perhaps it had all been in his head? Perhaps.

'Why don't we go camping?' Joe suggested.

'You're not afraid?' Louis asked.

'Hey, I thought you were supposed to be the adventurous one.' Winking at Louis, Joe said, 'I'm not afraid.'

Joe held out his hand on his lap and Louis clasped it. Just like they were eight again, running around the playground, holding hands and playing tag. The two friends sat on the swing chair, with the comforting touch of each other that only a reassuring hand hold can give.

'Thanks, Joe.' Louis said quietly, looking down onto the valley.

✻ ✻ ✻

They decided to camp. As they were nearly sixteen Louis's parents had agreed, then it was only a matter of persuasion to get Joe's parents to agree too. Besides, it was summer and a quiet alpine village.

What was the worst that could happen?

Joe and Louis had great fun unpacking their camping gear next to a very quiet and beautifully green clearing. The trees did look a little twisted, but Joe couldn't see much more than that.

They had a small camping stove and tins of beans to cook in the pan, matches for a campfire, a torch, and sleeping bags for their two-man tent. Both boys had also charged their phones, not only so that their parents could call them and check they were okay, but also to take videos and photos of the fairies when they came. Hopefully that night. Although, as Joe reasoned to Louis, they may have moved on. Perhaps they were travelling fairies?

Joe and Louis sat out by the campfire and looked out into the night. The stars above them were bright and clear, the moon hung in a little crescent and glowed softly cream. All around them the trees whispered and shuffled. Even if they didn't see fairies tonight, everything around them seemed enchanted, and that was almost enough to feed their imaginations.

Waiting until at least midnight, the boys watched the clearing carefully and chatted quietly. Deciding that the fairies had probably moved on, they put out the fire and snuggled up in the tent, to get a little rest before the sun rose.

It was quiet, dark and still, when Louis gently shook Joe awake. Placing his finger over Joe's mouth so that he didn't speak, Louis gently tugged at Joe, over to the tent door. Both boy's heads touched together at the bottom opening to the tent. Looking out, they saw the most wonderous, incredible sight.

In the middle of the clearing, not more than twenty metres away, the space was alive with little fairies. The clearing was lit by tiny lights in multi-colours and little dancing *people*, only they didn't quite look like people due to their thin willowy arms, very small size, and the addition of *wings* on their backs. There were many different types of fairies too: some were spindly and brown like twigs, some were green and spiky like the fir trees, and still others were as soft as the breeze, almost as if they were made from the air.

It was true then, there were fairies.

Joe and Louis watched what seemed to be some kind of fairy gathering, or fairy party. There was certainly a lot of dancing going on. Some fairies had taken the party to the air and were zipping around. Some were eating little wild strawberries while sat at miniature tables and, in their eager-ness to eat, they were standing on the table or each other and dripping strawberry juice on their neighbour's heads. Amongst the fairies one stood out. She was slightly taller than the others, her gown was longer and appeared to be made of sum-mer alpine flowers, and on her head, she wore a twisted crown, almost like twigs of gold encircling her head and protruding upwards from her long brown hair. From the crown fell little glass drop-lets, that looked like little drops of dew. Some of the fairies around her were bowing or kneeling, however most were trying to gain her attention. One bold fairy invited her to dance. It was the most beautiful thing the friends had ever seen. Without saying a word, the boys lay side by side, watching every enchanted moment.

Joe couldn't remember when he'd fallen asleep, but he awoke to the fresh morning air rolling over himself and Louis, where they lay side by side, the heads together at the entrance of the tent, Louis's protective arm draped over Joe.

Joe tried to stir without waking Louis and looked out at the empty clearing before them. They had seen it, hadn't they? It wasn't a figment of their imagination?

Louis stirred next to Joe. He pulled his arm off his friend's shoulders and looked around disorientated, until he remembered where they were, and looking at Joe, gave him a half-smile. 'You saw it too?' he asked.

Joe nodded to his friend in confirmation. 'Yes. I saw it.' he said. Then added, 'Completely nuts though.' Joe ran his fingers over his lips contemplating. Louis waited, knowing his friend had something important to say. Eventually, Joe said, 'Louis, I've seen it too. It is real. We did see fairies. But I don't think we should say anything to anyone else, not the other students at school or our parents. I just don't think they'd believe us.'

Louis followed his friend's thinking. 'Not a problem, Joe. Let's just keep it to ourselves.

Achily standing up from their bumpy ground mattress, the boys emerged from the tent and stumbled around outside. Louis wanted to start the camping stove, to make tea and some breakfast, but Joe wanted to investigate the clearing, and eventually Louis was persuaded to go with him.

There was a strange atmosphere, almost as if they were being watched. But looking around the boys could see they were the only ones in this part of the forest, certainly they couldn't see or hear other people.

Joe and Louis had a thorough search of the trees and the rabbit holes, amongst the grass and under logs. But they couldn't find anything. They were just about to return to the tent when Joe cried out to Louis, 'Stop! Don't put your foot down.' Louis obediently held his foot mid-step, while Joe dropped to his knees and, from under the sole of Louis's trainers, rescued a tiny, little, spiky gold ring, about the size of a thimble. He placed it in his palm for them both to inspect. It wasn't a ring; it was a small, twisted gold crown with delicate glass droplets as fine as the dew.

Joe looked around and said, 'Little fairies, I have your queen's crown.'

Everything stopped.

The air stood still, the breeze didn't move; birds stood motionless on the branches, their song halted while exiting their mouths. The clearing separated from reality and became its own bubble. There, before the boys, stood the Queen of the Fairies: Freya.

Queen Freya was dressed in a gown of silken cob-webs and drops of dew adorned her brown hair. Her face had fine features and she had grey eyes. Despite being so small, she was as gracious and magnanimous as any human queen.

Joe and Louis fell to their knees before her and Joe held out his hand, with the little crown resting carefully in the palm.

'Queen of the Fairies. I have found your crown.' Joe said. He averted his eyes as she came towards him.

'You may look upon me.' she said. Both boys raised their eyes. 'My name is Queen Freya.' She paused. 'You have done me a great service, Joe. I thank you. The fairies will always recognise you both as friends.' She reached forward and lifted her tiny crown from Joe's hand and placed it on her head. Then she continued, 'For your recognition of honesty, Joe, you will be granted the gift of joining us if ever you should choose. But I warn you. We live an enchanted life. If you join us,' and in so say-ing she indicated around her to the fairies that had gathered at the edge of the clearing and who were clamouring over each other in fascination and fear of the two boys, 'then, you may never return to your world. For once you enter the Kingdom of the Fairies, there is no return.'

What a strange thank you, Joe thought. But he was sensible, and recognised it was a kind offer, and that Queen Freya was likely quite powerful, so he carefully replied, 'Thank you, Queen Freya, I am honoured.'

The world took a breath and started again. The clearing was as it was before. Nothing remarkable except a few twisted trees and a patch of vivid green grass.

Joe and Louis turned to each other; their eyes locked in their secret. Without saying a word, each knew that they must keep this to themselves.

* * *

With the return to school at the end of the summer the weather turned and so did Joe and Louis's fate, none of it for the better. Not only was it the last year before their exams, but a new kid had joined from the city, and he was really, really unpleasant.

Most of Joe and Louis's friends recognised and respected their deep friendship. Just as cones belonged to pine trees, everyone accepted Joe and Louis as belonging together. It was perfectly natural and nothing strange. However, Tom, the new boy was a spiteful troublemaker, who liked to believe he was incredibly intelligent and important, and to cover that he wasn't, instead had become a horrible bully. Or worse. There were rumours.

Tom had had to leave the city rather quickly. His parents had whisked him away, and this was not the first time. Tom started at the school innocently enough, charming the teachers and wooing the girls, while trying to impress the boys, telling them that he "stood by his word" and he was a boy of "honour and loyalty", but nothing could be further from the truth. It wasn't long before his true colours started to show.

Noticing Joe and Louis were so close, Tom decided to play games on them. This was little more than a reaction to his own jealousy that he had never had a real friendship and he was incapable of feeling love. Rather than reflecting on why, Tom accosted Louis in the corridor and said, 'I heard Joe say you were stupid. He pretends to you that you're not, but he has to correct your homework and everyone knows.'

Louis shrugged Tom off and walked away in the opposite direction.

Tom tried his luck on Joe. Running in next to Joe after sports, Tom said, 'Louis told me you are so boring. You never do anything exciting. I can't think why he'd say that about you. Can you?'

Joe ignored Tom.

But Tom hadn't finished yet. He wanted his emotional reaction. He wanted to split their friendship and make them feel pain, because pain was the only emotion Tom was able to feel. Changing tactic, Tom singled them out in class, saying aloud to their classmates, 'Don't you think it's odd how they *always* sit together?' or, 'I saw them whispering *really close*.' or, 'Most boys I know are interested in girls not boys.' Eventually a girl at the back of the class told Tom to shut up. But this just burnt his ego and pushed him further.

Tom watched Joe and Louis incessantly. It was tough for the boys to be constantly under his glare. One day, in mid-December, just before they were about to break for Christmas (and Louis shouldn't have done it, but he just needed reassurance from Joe after a particularly nasty session of catcalling from Tom) Louis brushed the back of Joe's hand as they left the class and said in a low voice just between them, 'Fairies.' It was Louis's way of feeling that they had a bond and a secret that was unbreakable, despite Tom's bullying. Louis didn't know, but Tom had seen and he had heard.

Tom took Joe and Louis's bus back from school that day. He was a menacing black presence at the back of the bus. The boys tried to ignore him as they sat together and watched the snow-covered slopes while the bus slowly wound its way up the road to home. When the bus reached the little alpine village, all the remaining children alighted, including Tom. Joe and Louis started to make their way home.

Joe and Louis could feel Tom behind them, like an evil, dark cloud, so desperate to belong, so detached from real human love, that he had to take away other's pleasure and feed off their pain in a triumphant display of dominance. Because Tom's cup could never be full, he repeated the cycle everywhere he went. Five schools now. And worse.

Joe and Louis hunched over together, and whispered in low tones, as they pulled their puffy jackets tighter and held the straps of their rucksacks.

Thump. A snowball came hurtling through the air and hit Louis on the back of the head.

Joe turned around angrily to face Tom, not more than five metres behind them and said, 'Cut it out. Go home Tom. You are not wanted here.'

Tom raised his arm in anger and took aim again, only this time it wasn't a snowball, it was a rock.

Joe ducked and the rock narrowly missed his head, shattering a car window behind him.

Louis's eyes were wide with fear. He grabbed Joe's jacket and shouted, 'Run!'

Run the boys did. Up the road, past the gate, up the lane. Ahead of them stood Louis's parents chalet. His parents wouldn't be home for at least another half an hour, and Louis didn't think he could get the key out in time. So, the boys kept running. Up, up, up. Into the alpine woods that they knew so well.

Behind them, Tom followed. His eyes wide and thirsty for the hunt.

They were high in the tree line now. The snow was thick and deep. Joe would have run forever, but Louis tripped, slipped, and fell a little way.

'Louis!' Joe called, and immediately ran to the aid of his friend. But not before Tom got to him first.

Clutching at Louis's beautiful white-blonde hair, Tom dragged him up by it and pinned him against a tree. Louis had a trickle of blood down the side of his face and cried out in pain as Tom dropped a fistful of hair onto the crisp white snow.

Joe picked up a stick and directly faced Tom, not more than a few metres away.

Tom had his arm over Louis's neck, in his other hand he held a large, steel, hunting knife.

'Joe, no!' Louis called from his captivity. His eyes straining in fear to protect his friend.

'Now isn't this interesting?' Tom salivated. His black soulless eyes drunk on their fear. 'Two little fairies in a woodland.'

Joe measured the weight of the stick in his hand and made his calculations.

Tom continued, 'So you have a choice, Joe. Say you love Louis and I might let him go. Say you don't and I'll slit his silly white throat. It isn't the first time.'

The words hung like poison in the air. The boys had no doubt that Tom was capable of killing, they knew that they would never have any peace. The ultimatum meant nothing; it was a baseless sham. Very likely someone was about to get hurt or worse. This was just a twisted game to Tom. Louis also knew that Joe would never abandon him.

Joe and Louis's eyes connected. Louis knew. Louis opened his mouth as if to say . . .

'Freya!' said Joe.

Time stopped.

The breeze stopped. The snow stopped falling. Everyone and everything was still. Except Joe and Freya, Queen of the Fairies.

Queen Freya stood before him in a gown of fluffy, soft snow. On her head was a crown of pure ice, shaped like little icicles dripping up into the heavens. 'Joe?' she said.

Joe dropped to the ground before her. 'Queen Freya. You once made me an offer. You once said to me that I was a friend of the fairies. I need your friendship now. You once said to me that I could come and join you in the enchanted fairy kingdom. Dear Queen Freya, could Louis and I come join you now?'

'You can, but the invitation was only for you, Joe. Not Louis.' Queen Freya looked a little sad.

'May I?' Joe said. He reached out his hand to her tiny one and placed her hand on his heart. 'Louis is my only love. I cannot live a life without him. I beg you, my generous Queen. Feel my heart. Show us pity.'

A small tear escaped from Queen Freya's eye as she felt his warm heart, only moments away from breaking and stopping forever. 'Very well.' she said. 'But this will be for eternity. You will never be able to go back.'

'I would rather spend an eternity with my only love, caught in your enchanted kingdom, than a lifetime in this lonely world without him. I am sure.' Joe said.

'Go gather your friend, carry him with you, and follow me.' Queen Freya commanded.

Joe stood and carefully navigated his way through the snow, to where Louis and Tom's motionless bodies stood. Tom's black eyes were boring into Louis's terrified cry to Joe. Joe shivered in the presence of pure evil. Gently lifting the knife blade and arm back from Louis's neck, Joe slid Louis out, lifted him heavily over his shoulder, and stumbled back to where the Fairy Queen and her growing entourage stood.

'Follow me.' Queen Freya commanded. The entourage started to move up the hill, some flying, some walking, all in hushed tones. Taking one last glance behind him, Joe saw the shadow of Louis's body on the snow, red blood splattered around him, Tom's mouth open in some kind of blood thirsty war cry. Joe's almost shape still standing with a stick in his hand. But it wasn't really Joe and Louis, because they had gone.

Up, up, up the hill. Louis's weight was heavy and Joe struggled and strained through the snow, but as he walked little fairies came to his aid, flying all around him and holding parts of Louis's clothing. After what seemed like a long, long time they finally reached the clearing. No longer green and lush, no longer dotted by wild strawberries and alpine flowers, but covered in snow. Gently dropping Louis in the centre of the clearing, Joe fell down exhausted beside him, cradling Louis's head on his lap. Joe felt the world breathe again.

Just like a watercolour being painted, the world around Joe started to fill in. It was wonderous.

The snow sparkled like glitter and the trees were lit with little multicoloured lights. Tiny fairy homes dotted the trees, they were connected by little walkways, and little ladders from their homes fell to ground. There were fairies dancing and singing. Fairies were flying around them and touching Joe and Louis in wonder.

Queen Freya pointed to a particularly large tree a little way back from the clearing with a huge hole at its base. In many ways it reminded Joe of the opening to their tent this summer just gone. A lifetime ago. 'You can live there.' she said. 'It may not look like much, but remember our homes are magical and we are not bound by space and time. Once you descend the stairs, I think you will find it more than comfortable.' Looking up at Joe, she said, 'Now Joe, you must wake your friend.'

'But how?' asked Joe, cradling Louis in his arms, 'Please tell me how?'

'You wake him with true love's kiss.' Queen Freya replied.

Joe tenderly leant over his friend and kissed him awake.

9. SECRET SANTA

Sarah had worked at Port Enterprise for nearly two years. After the office reorganisation Sarah had to change groups and was placed at a desk next to Kevan. Sarah had sat next to Kevan for nine months, three weeks and two days. And she had been madly in love with him for nine months, three weeks and one day.

Kevan was tall, with dark-blonde hair and sparkling blue eyes. He was intelligent and kind. He had a warm sense of humour which was reflected in his eyes. Kevan liked motorbikes and travelling. He would give people his undivided attention, stopping his work, turning to them, and tuning the world out. It was a charming trait. Quite simply, to Sarah, Kevan was perfect. It's just that he would never know how Sarah felt, because she could never tell him.

Sarah had hazel eyes and red hair. She hated the curl in her hair, so she tried to straighten it every morning before work using an expensive straightening brush. It was the only luxury ten minutes of time she allowed herself, as she was a busy mum to a darling little boy and the mornings were always a rush. In all other aspects, Sarah was ordinary:

kind, gentle, softly spoken, average height, average weight. In many ways Sarah felt her son was her greatest achievement.

Every day, Sarah diligently turned up to work, did her job, left at the same time every evening, picked up her son and snuggled up with him at home. In nearly every way, Sarah was content and happy. She could afford her bills and her little boy was her world. But one day he would grow up. As much as Sarah didn't consciously realise it, her son, Connor needed a good father figure, and Sarah very much needed a kind, stable partner to share her world with.

Each morning, Sarah arrived at the same time to her desk at work. Kevan was always there before her. Typing away on some report or another.

'Morning Sarah!' Kevan turned and greeted her with a kind smile.

'Morning Kevan.' Sarah replied with her own warm smile. Apart from picking up her son from school, this was her next favourite moment of the day.

Sarah settled herself down at her desk, logged in, checked the most urgent emails, then left for a coffee from the coffee bean machine. Settling herself back at her desk, Kevan turned to Sarah and they had their usual brief morning conversation about the news, or some amusing email from an imploding member of staff, or some funny story from Connor the night before.

For a few minutes every day, Sarah and Kevan

entered their happy bubble. Sometimes Kevan wanted to show Sarah something on his computer screen and she got to move closer, inches away from him, as she craned to look where he directed. They'd once touched hands when she passed a leaving card to Kevan for him to sign, their eyes connected and they'd shared a brief moment. But nothing had come of it. Sarah had lived on the moment of that touch for at least a week. As with all of these little moments and unsaid words though, nothing had come of it.

* * *

Christmas was just a few weeks away, and Abagail (whom Sarah didn't like that much – although she couldn't quite put her finger on why) suggested that their group do a secret Santa this year. The idea was to put their names on pieces of paper, which were put into a pot, then pull out a different name, and get that person an amusing Christmas gift for under ten pounds. They'd open their secret Santa presents just before their team Christmas lunch, which was organised at a nearby pub and booked just before they all left for their Christmas holidays.

The team thought it was a fun idea and excitedly wrote their names on bits of paper to put into the pot. Abagail pulled out a piece of paper first, without checking herself, she rolled her eyes in annoyance, then quickly covering the act, she smiled and said, too brightly, 'Oh! I know exactly what to get this person!'

Kevan was next, he raised his eyebrows as he read the name, then refolded the paper. Sarah pulled her paper and read: Darren Waterhouse. Darren handled the project management for the team. She'd have to think of something funny, but her mind went blank. Refolding the paper, she resolved that inspiration would come to her later.

Abagail bounded around the members of their team, who were sat at their desks, with her little pot of names. The team numbered twelve in total. The last person to take a name was their boss, Lewis Murray. He smiled and gave a hearty laugh as he saw the name. Then he thanked Abagail, and the team settled back to work. Only, most of team were actually surreptitiously checking online websites for whoopie cushions and joke flowers for at least the next half an hour.

Not long afterwards, Kevan got up and invited Abagail for a coffee in the breakout room. Sarah looked on with muted jealously. She tried to reason with herself that it was his choice to have a coffee with whomsoever he chose, she just wished it was her.

* * *

Sarah spent Sunday afternoon writing a Christmas letter to Santa with her son Connor. His list was fairly extensive, so she reminded him that Santa didn't buy everything on the list.

'Okay, Mummy. Can I put some stickers by the one I really want?' Connor asked.

'That's a good idea sweetheart.' Sarah said.

Deliberately, Connor placed stickers next to the "Astrohero Space Rocket" which was number three on his list and carefully written in his best writing. Sarah craned her head over his shoulder and made a mental note of the list. She'd already got most of the items but not the rocket toy. She'd need to look for it during her coffee break at work tomorrow. Luckily, work was happy to take in personal parcel deliveries. As long as Sarah ordered it now, it would be delivered in good time for Christmas.

Happily, Connor sealed the letter, and together they wrapped up in coats and gloves against the cold, to go and post it.

Connor grabbed his scooter, while Sarah held his special letter to Santa. Together they posted the letter in the red postbox at the end of their road. Giving Connor a high five, mother and son walked on to the park so that Connor could ride his scooter. It was a perfect Sunday afternoon.

✳ ✳ ✳

When Sarah arrived at work the next day, she found that Abagail had been busy decorating their desks. Most monitors were covered in tinsel, and little baubles hung from their desk lamps. It really was a kind thing to do; Sarah really couldn't understand why Abagail got under her skin.

'Morning Sarah!' Kevan turned and greeted her with a kind smile.

'Morning Kevan.' Sarah replied with her own warm smile and sat down at her desk. She logged in to her computer to check the most urgent emails. After she'd dealt with them, she got up for her coffee, and upon her return she and Kevan had their usual morning chat.

'How was your weekend?' Kevan asked Sarah.

'Oh, it was lovely thanks. Connor and I were writing his letter together to Santa. He's doing so well with his writing. Connor really wants an "Astro-hero Space Rocket" this year, so I'll need to order it later today to make sure "Santa" is able to gift it in time for Christmas.' she said.

Kevan smiled. 'I wish I still believed in Santa. I know exactly what's on my wish list this year!' and smiled a secret smile to himself. He continued, 'I remember that feeling I got as a kid when I saw the stocking full of toys. It felt so magical.' He smiled wistfully at the memory. Then reconnecting his eyes with Sarah, he said, 'You're a great mum you know. Connor is lucky to have you.'

Sarah shook her head. 'I worry. He sometimes feels like he's missing out by not having a father like the other children at school. I try to list all his classmates that only have mums and not dads, but it doesn't help. The idealised Christmas family films don't help too. So, I try to be everything I can to him. Mum guilt I guess.'

Kevan tried to reassure her. 'You don't have to be everything to him. You are enough. He's a lucky little boy. It may look like everyone else has it sorted, but everyone has their difficulties, they just don't let it show. Think of the families where the dad is a drunk or abusive, think of the children that have lost both parents. There's a wide rainbow of normal when it comes to families.' Kevan had turned his chair towards her as per normal and was giving her his undivided attention. He continued, 'Just so you know. I think you do a great job.'

Sarah smiled, 'Thanks, Kevan, it really means a lot.' Sarah turned back to her work, and exhaled, trying to let go of feeling not good enough.

* * *

Later that day, Sarah took a five-minute break to grab another coffee and search online for the coveted rocket toy. Much to her disappointment the first few online stores she checked were already sold out. Sarah clicked her tongue in annoyance and Kevan looked up from his work.

Sarah checked a some more, smaller, online stores. Then did a general search. *Click, click, click.* Her desperation started to escape her, as she made little noises of annoyance. Finally, she said out loud, 'Ugh. This is so frustrating!'

'Anything I can help you with?' Kevan looked over kindly at her.

'It's nothing.' Sarah said, shaking her head.

'Really? Problem shared is a problem halved.' Kevan persisted.

Sarah hesitated, then said, 'Connor really wants this rocket toy from Santa. I didn't realise it was going to be such an issue, but apparently, it's in high-demand and it's sold out. I can't find it anywhere.'

'Oh?' Kevan said with concern, looking over at her computer. 'What's it called?'

'Astrohero Space Rocket.' Sarah replied. She tried to hide her frustration.

'Let me have a check.' Kevan kindly offered, as he tapped the details into his search engine and clicked a few different sites. Sarah looked over hopefully, but Kevan's search was fruitless. 'I can't seem to find it in stock either.' he said sadly. 'I'm really sorry. You never know. They may release more stock in a week or so. Perhaps keep checking the websites?'

'Yes.' said Sarah dejectedly. 'Thanks for looking, Kevan. I really appreciate it.'

'Anytime.' said Kevan looking thoughtful. He rubbed his fingers over his lips and returned to his work.

❊ ❊ ❊

The next couple of weeks continued to prove fruitless in the search for the coveted rocket toy, which apparently was the number one wanted toy this Christmas. Sarah had a horrible sinking feeling in her heart. She really felt like she was letting Connor down.

Sarah confided in Kevan how awful she was feeling. How she felt like a failed mum. He tried to reassure her as best he could.

Their boss Lewis walked by. 'Everything okay, Sarah?' he asked.

'Absolutely, Lewis! All going well. The Morgan report is nearly finished and I'll have it on your desk by close of business today.' Sarah brightly replied.

'Great!' Lewis said and looked pleased at both Sarah and Kevan. They were great members of the team. No trouble at all.

After Lewis left, Sarah said in a quiet whisper to Kevan, 'I've been so preoccupied with this rocket toy, I'd also completely forgotten about the secret Santa. I really need to get something. Our team lunch is in two days. How about you?'

Kevan smiled at her. 'Secret Santa? I've just about got that sorted. It's taken a bit of work.' He smiled widely to himself as he tapped away at his keyboard. Sarah raised a quizzical eyebrow to him but he didn't say anything else.

Abagail bounded over to them and commanded Kevan's attention regarding a work issue. So, Sarah turned back to her work and tried to tune them out.

* * *

The team were excited as it was the day of their

annual Christmas team lunch. But Sarah was finding it hard during the morning to join in with the cheery Christmas spirit. All she could think about was Connor's disappointment when Santa didn't get him the toy he wanted this Christmas.

This was the first Christmas lunch Sarah had attended with the team since joining, and overall, she really enjoyed being in the group. Sarah had finally decided on a funny daily diary for Darren as his secret Santa gift. He liked planning, so a diary to organise his time would fit well. On each day was a humorous motivational message, such as: "You can't have everything, you don't have the desk space." or, "I always aspired to be somebody one day. I realise now I should have been more specific." Sarah had wrapped it in suitably Christmassy paper and handed it to Abagail before lunch.

The team started putting on their coats and grabbing their bags for their lunch out. Abagail bounded over to Kevan and fawned at his arm. 'Kevan, the Santa sack is a little big. Would you carry it for me?' Sarah looked down at her locked computer screen and tried not to feel annoyed at Abagail touching Kevan.

The team walked to the pub. Sarah walked with Kevan at the back of the group. He was carrying the enormous black bin bag of gifts. There were only twelve of them in the team, so it was surprising the amount of presents secret Santa had generated. Sarah wondered if her present for Darren was enough, but Abagail had clearly stipulated a gift value up to ten pounds. Anyway, it was a secret, no one would know.

Kevan sat across the table from Sarah at lunch, and much to Sarah's annoyance Abagail placed herself right next to him. The rest of the team filed around the long, oblong, sticky, pub table, decorated with festive candles and cheap, red-and-green Christmas crackers.

Lewis, their boss, stood up and gave a brief speech about fantastic team spirit and all the hard work they'd put in this year. He then looked gratefully over at Abagail for her excellent idea of the team Christmas secret Santa this year.

Excitedly, Abagail stood up and went to the black bin bag she'd placed in the corner, to start distributing the presents around. Jingly Christmas music played in the background of the pub as the team sipped drinks and waited to be passed their secret Santa present.

Presents were distributed around the group to much hilarity and the ripping of paper. Lewis, their boss, was given a pair of pink, furry handcuffs. Most of the team laughed, some a little uncertainty. Sarah tried to look away, but it seemed that their boss had taken the joke well and was laughing heartily at the end of the table. *Phew.*

From the bag, Abagail withdrew a huge box, wrapped in blue penguin paper. Abagail looked a little annoyed as she said, 'This one is for you, Sarah.'

'Oh!' Sarah replied. 'It's huge.' She looked a little embarrassed as team members helped Abagail pass it over to Sarah.

'Open it!' one of her colleagues shouted over to her.

With a puzzled brow, Sarah started to rip off the wrapping paper and revealed . . .

'An Astrohero Space Rocket!' Sarah said. She couldn't believe it. Her hands shook slightly as she turned the box around in her hands and checked inside to make sure it was the real thing.

'That's an odd present.' Abagail said and shot an angry look at Kevan next to her.

Sarah looked up to see Abagail looking cross, and Kevan looking directly at her.

Lewis, their boss, shouted down the table, 'You planning on a career change?' Most of the team laughed. Sarah shook her head "No." and carefully placed her gift under the table. From across the table Abagail looked as if she'd eaten a lemon.

It was, quite frankly, the best gift Sarah had ever received. It was almost as if someone knew. Sarah shot a few looks at Kevan during lunch, but he didn't say anything. Sarah looked over at her boss, Lewis. Perhaps it was him? Sarah looked around her team. It could be anyone really, except Abagail. Whoever it was, Sarah was grateful.

The team returned to work after lunch in high spirits. Sarah hadn't realised how stressed and worried she'd been about the rocket toy, she finally felt she was able to relax and laugh along with the Christmas spirit. Carefully placing the present under her desk at work, Sarah went to get a coffee. Kevan had popped down to the mail room to collect something, and Abagail was typing furiously at her desk.

Returning from the tearoom, Sarah happily sat down and logged in to her computer. Taking one last glance under her desk at the coveted rocket toy, to her horror, Sarah saw it was gone!

✳ ✳ ✳

Sarah felt physically sick. Within the space of a couple of hours she'd gone from feeling completely rubbish at not being able to source the rocket toy, to elation and joy at the Christmas spirit, that someone knew and had been kind enough to buy it for her to give to her son, then, in the worst possible turn of bad luck, someone else had taken it. Sarah looked around her team and behind her at the rest of the office. Who would do such a mean thing?

Sarah crouched down on her hands and knees under her desk, just in case the large box had been pushed aside. From behind her she heard Kevan say, 'Looking for this?'

Sarah scrambled up from the floor. She saw Kevan standing over her, holding the lost Astro-hero Space Rocket box. 'Oh, my goodness.' she said. 'You found it! What happened? Where was it?'

Kevan set his mouth to a hard line. 'I'd ordered

some specialist motorbike wheels. I went down to the mail room to collect them and went out the back door of the mail room to take them to the car. I found Abagail out back, about to throw this into the skip.'

'What?' Sarah said.

'She said you'd asked her to get rid of the box. So, I checked it, but I found the toy was still inside. I thought you might still want it.'

Sarah gratefully clutched the box to her. 'Thank you!' she said tearfully. 'Thank you so much. You don't know what this means to me.' In relief, Sarah shakily sat down and carefully placed the box beside her.

Abagail suddenly rushed over to them saying, 'Oh Sarah, I tried to dispose of that box as you asked me to. But Kevan wanted it.' She gave a high-pitched laugh.

Sarah replied, 'I didn't ask you to dispose of the box.'

'Yes, you did.' Abagail asserted. 'Perhaps you have forgotten. You must have meant a different box.'

'No.' said Sarah coldly.

'Oh well. No harm done.' Abagail replied.

Sarah and Kevan exchanged glances and Kevan said, 'I have an idea, Sarah. Why don't I take this down to my car, and drop it off to you tonight when Connor has gone to bed.'

Sarah looked at him gratefully. 'Oh, that would be really kind. Thank you.' she replied.

Abagail could hardly contain her rage as she

blurted out, 'Well just so you know it was Kevan that bought you the secret Santa present anyway.' Sourness stained her face as she stared at Sarah. 'I don't think it is very good. He asked me to change secret Santa names, so I did. Just so you know I don't really think it is part of the team spirit. In fact, I think it's odd and perhaps I ought to talk to Lewis about it.'

'That's right,' said Kevan, 'I changed out names for our boss, Lewis. Whom I believe you bought pink, furry handcuffs. I don't think his wife will be pleased if she was to find that out?'

Abagail stood for a few seconds in repressed rage. Unable to think of anything profound she finally managed a fake smile and said, 'I don't think I'll do secret Santa next year. Happy Christmas!' before flouncing off.

Sarah was shocked. She'd always had a bad feeling about Abagail, but she still couldn't believe she'd do something like that. Connor was just a kid. What she did was mean.

Kevan broke her thoughts by picking up the much-valued toy and saying, 'I hope it's okay? What time to you want me to come around tonight?'

Looking over at Kevan with love and gratitude in her eyes, Sarah said, 'Would eight p.m. be okay?'

Kevan smiled, 'That would be perfect. See you tonight.' And left for his car with the present safely under his arm.

* * *

Sarah put Connor to bed, brushed her teeth, refreshed her makeup, and tried not to feel excited as she waited for Kevan to knock on the door. She didn't know what was going to happen, but somehow she felt things had changed. Secrets weren't secrets anymore. Perhaps she'd be brave enough to tell Kevan how she felt. Sarah sat in the sitting room of her little terraced house, waiting. She was a bundle of nerves.

At a few minutes past eight there was a knock at the door. Checking out of her bay window, Sarah could see Kevan in the light from the streetlights. It felt strange to see someone she knew so well in a different location. Excitedly, Sarah rushed around to the door to open it.

Sarah ushered Kevan inside her house and gratefully received the rocket toy. She was so incredibly lucky! Sarah breathed a big sigh of relief and said, 'Thank you so much, Kevan for driving over tonight, you don't know what this means to me.'

Kevan raised an eyebrow at her. 'Actually, I think I do. I do sit next to you every day.'

Sarah smiled and continued, 'I really appreciate it. And you swapped secret Santa names with Abagail. I'm surprised she agreed, how did you know she had my name?'

'Err.' Kevan replied.

'Kevan?'

'Err. Well, to be completely honest . . .' Kevan looked nervously at his feet as he stood in Sarah's hallway. 'Err. Too much university poker?' Sarah looked confused, so Kevan continued, 'I got the sense Abagail didn't like you that much, so when she pulled a name out the pot and rolled her eyes, I correctly guessed it was your name. As I had Lewis's name, I guessed she'd much prefer to try and score points with the boss than buy something for you. So, I took a gamble and I was right.'

'But you didn't know about the rocket toy at that point. I didn't tell you until after.' Sarah said, a puzzled expression still over her brow.

'No. That's right. You didn't.' Kevan looked even more embarrassed as he decided to make a clean breast of it. 'In truth I wanted to get you a secret Santa present. I wasn't initially intending to get one for Connor, but then I saw how worried and upset you were and I thought you'd much prefer this. I hope you don't mind.'

Sarah smiled widely at him, and said, 'I don't mind at all. The gift is perfect. You have really made my Christmas.'

'I have?' Kevan said hopefully.

Bravely, Sarah said, 'I don't suppose you'd like to stop for a while, for a tea or coffee or something?'

Kevan smiled adoringly at Sarah, 'Thank you, I'd like that very much.'

For the first time, in what would be a ritual that would be repeated hundreds of times in their future life together, Sarah went through to the kit-

chen to put on the kettle and make a cup of tea for
Kevan.

10. LORD ASHCROFT'S LAST LOVE

Lord Ashcroft was the epitome of proper. He'd served in the military and survived. He married well and worked in banking for a time, before returning when his dear father died to the family estate in Cornwall with his wife and children. He managed the estate well and was fair and just to all the tenants. Lord Ashcroft didn't lose money or gain much money, rather he preserved and maintained. Everything was just as it should be, except, he'd never been in love.

When Lord Ashcroft had met his wife at the age of thirty-two, it was because his father had told him, 'Son, it is time for you to marry.' As Lord Ashcroft was tall and good looking, with light-brown hair, a moustache and sparkling hazel eyes, he hadn't found it too difficult to attract a good wife. So, with the same stoic perseverance that Lord Ashcroft had applied to every aspect of his life, he found someone suitable and non-offensive, married and had children.

Lord Ashcroft's three children were his world, and while he did grow very fond of his wife, it was never the heart stopping romance that he read about, secretly, in the books of his library. Lord Ashcroft's favourite secret passion was to sneak down to the library with a bottle of port and read late into the night. He'd read all the romantic classics. His heart had soared with joy when Mr Darcy finally declared his unwavering love for Elizabeth Bennet *in the right way*. He'd wept when Heathcliff ran to the bedroom to be haunted by Catherine for all eternity. And, oh, how the line, "All the sunshine I can feel is in her presence" had stayed with him for weeks after he'd read it. He thought at the time his sobbing might have woken his family, so he'd placed his hand over his mouth and let the hot tears flow. Dear Jane! Lord Ashcroft had read about and felt true love with every cell in his body, which was why he knew he had never been in love with his wife, or anyone else.

As the years passed his hair grew grey and his face became lined and wrinkled. Slowly his back started to stoop and he found he couldn't walk quite so far with the dogs anymore. One by one his children left to follow their stars and eventually it was just him and his wife in the large, draughty, old manor.

Buxton Manor was an old sprawling mediaeval manor on the edge of Bodmin Moor. The original part of the building had a huge dining hall, with large open hearths either side, and little hidden windows below the rafters, connecting to secret passageways and hidden rooms. People were very suspicious in those days. Then, through the ages, the building had been "improved" with modern additions, each one stamping its own particular style on the manor, and not concerned about matching the rest. There was an Elizabethan walled garden; Georgian façade with three-metre-high, large, square rooms behind; Edwardian stables and a Victorian orangery. Somehow the patchwork quilt of architectural styles were successfully connected using wonky corridors and strange, little, half-height doors. It was unusual, but it was home.

Sadly, the winter after their last child left home, Lord Ashcroft's wife died. It had been a particularly bad influenza season and the pneumonia just wouldn't shift.

Loyally, Lord Ashcroft stayed at her bedside holding her hand to the end. It was like saying goodbye to an old and faithful friend. He held up through the funeral, gratefully accepted people's kind condolences, consoled his children until they returned to their lives, then shut the manor door and was alone.

* * *

Lady Ashcroft had never been the love of his life, but now that he was left to his own devices, Lord Ashcroft found that he didn't cope very well. He started eating jam out of the jar with a spoon. Or cold baked beans because he just couldn't be bothered to heat them and add the toast. Sometimes he only washed once a week because he didn't care if his tenants thought he was smelly, and he really couldn't be bothered. What was it all for?

Lord Ashcroft took a long hard look at himself in the large, speckled hall mirror and to his shock, he saw and old, bent man staring back at him. He could accept that he was aging, he understood the concept, but his heart was sad that he would close this life having never really loved.

Lord Ashcroft's children were a little worried that their father wasn't taking care of himself. So, they held a family council. Richard, Prudence and Hugo decided they would engage a housekeeper from the village on the pretence of them all visiting over Christmas (knowing he wouldn't be able to cope without help), then persuade her to stay with the threat to their father that they would come again.

Prue had the task to find the housekeeper. Prue was practical and astute, but she'd also inherited her father's romantic inclinations. She was more than happy to be assigned the task by the family to find a housekeeper. She knew in her heart just what she had to do.

* * *

Prue took two weeks off work, and made a special trip down to Cornwall, to find a housekeeper for her father.

Sitting in her little bed and breakfast (she didn't want her father to know their plan until completion) Prue made a list of the qualities she was looking for in a housekeeper: kind, warm, loving, fun (as long as it matched her father's sense of humour that would be enough) and could cook. Prudence thought a little, it was already a long list, but she squeezed in one more trait: feminine.

'Okay,' Prue said to herself, 'I'm not going to find all those traits in the local village. I'm going to need to get creative. Where can I find such a woman? Then inspiration hit her. She knew exactly where she had to look.

❊ ❊ ❊

Prue parked up the car at her first destination. It was seven thirty in the evening and she was famished. The locals had recommended the establishment highly. Prue had great hopes.

Walking towards the pub, Prue could see that it was busy, mainly with bikers. Prue tried not to be judgemental as she entered. Walking up to the bar she could see the landlord and landlady were busy serving drinks. The bikers were thirsty and potentially hungry, and Prue was at the back of the queue. There was also a bar lady trying her best to help out. Noticing the landlady had a wedding ring on her finger, Prue turned her attention to the bar lady. She was in her late forties, a little curvy, had her hair cut very short and had dyed it black.

She wore a leopard V-neck top and had a leather cord around her neck with a shark's tooth on it. Still, Prue persevered. She really wanted to be open in her search, particularly as money really makes such a difference when it comes to appearance.

Prue watched the lady for at least ten minutes, then she decided to try a little test. Leaning forward on her bar stool, she said to the bar lady, 'Excuse me? Excuse me?' the bar lady tried to ignore her, so Prue tried again. She certainly got a response.

'Look love. You can see I'm busy. I'm sorry, but you're going to have to wait and if that don't suit you then find somewhere else to drink.' Dramatically, the lady flapped a tea towel over her shoulder to emphasise her busyness, turned her back on Prue and walked to the other end of the bar.

Prue thought to herself, "Oh, no, no, no. That won't do at all. Not very kind." So, Prue left.

Prue reached the next pub at a little after eight. Her tummy grumbled but she tried to focus on the task. This pub was a little quieter and a little posher. No motorbikes, no unusual jewellery. Prue felt a little more hopeful as she walked through the door.

The landlord had a bar lady and a bar man helping him, as well as a chef in the back. The area to the right was cordoned off as a family area and had a pool table and some fruit machines. There were a couple of tourist families finishing their evening meals and some children, aged between eight and twelve, Prue guessed, playing at the pool table. One of the mums also had a small baby, possibly from a second marriage (Prue correctly assumed).

Prue sat herself down at the bar and the bar lady came to greet her. 'What can I get you love?'

'Oh, just a soda and lime, and the bar menu thank you.' Prue watched the lady prepare her drink. She was small and skinny, her skin was a little wrinkly but in a sunny and tanned sort of way. Around her neck she wore several gold chains, and had on a pretty georgette blouse. All okay so far.

The bar lady returned with her drink, and as the bar wasn't too full, Prue tried to engage the lady in a little light conversation. Prue hadn't got far when the little baby in the family area woke up and started to cry out in distress.

The bar lady winced with discomfort and shot an angry look at the family. The baby continued to cry and fuss. The bar lady pressed her finger to her ear and said, 'Sorry love. Can't hear a word you're saying.' She shot another annoyed look at the family and muttered, 'Bars are no place for children.' before giving a look of distain and heading off into the kitchens out back.

"Oh dear!" Pure thought. "That's not very warm or loving." Shaking her head, Prue left and headed back to the village where her bed and breakfast was located. Parking up in the square, she headed for the nearest pub. It was twenty to nine in the evening. She walked over to the bar to ask for a bar menu.

'Sorry,' the landlord said, 'food finishes at eight-thirty.'

Prue's tummy grumbled. She smiled her nicest smile, 'Could you make an exception? I'm famished.'

The bar man looked a little annoyed but appreciated Prue's kind smile. 'Let me check with the chef love. I can't promise a yes.' he disappeared around the back.

Prue looked around the pub while she waited. Dark-stained oak was everywhere, there were white painted walls and red upholstered seats and banquettes. Overall, the effect was somewhere between cosy and dramatic. There was a pool table at the far end with a crowd having a match, and a dart board the other end which looked well used. The bar itself was covered with the usual beer mats advertising this or that local brew, it wasn't too sticky. Just the normal.

From behind the bar came the chef. She had her hair tied back in a ponytail and her hair was dyed dark red. She looked like she was in her early fifties. She wore a floral V-neck jumper and jeans under her apron. She was slightly above average height and had a good curve to her figure. She looked normal. She walked over to Prue.

Prue said, 'I'm so sorry, I know you've just stopped food. I'm famished. Is there anything you could give me? I'd be so grateful.'

The lady smiled kindly, 'I've just turned the friers off love, so no chips. I could do you a steak and kidney pie with boiled potatoes and vegetables?'

'I'm vegetarian.' Prue said, wincing.

'What about a nice macaroni cheese?' the lady suggested.

'Sounds delicious.' Prue replied.

'Done.' the lady said. Then added, 'Don't forget you owe me a favour!' and winked at her good-naturedly. Prue quite liked her.

Prue waited patiently for the chef to bring her food out to the table. When she arrived, Prue tried her best to engage her in conversation. As the lady had finished cooking for the night, she had a brief chat with Prue. Prue discovered she had two children who were grown up and living in Australia, she was divorced and she cooked for the pub. Prue could hear the *ping, ping, ping* in her head as the list ticked off. Prue resolved to return tomorrow with an offer the lady couldn't refuse.

❋ ❋ ❋

Lord Ashcroft was speechless when Prue arrived up the drive with his new housekeeper. He didn't want to accuse his daughter and sons of being interfering. But she was. He tried to remain polite as he showed Violet (the lady Prue had "discovered" at the pub) around, and enquired privately with Prue what the arrangement would be.

'Eighteen months, Dad. Then she has to go to Australia to be with her sons. This job will help pay for it. She can cook and she is nice. Plus, she is happy to accommodate this Christmas and next Christmas before she leaves in the January following for Australia. As her family are in Australia, she can be here the Christmas seasons. She has Wednesday afternoon and Saturday off.' Prue said.

Lord Ashcroft replied, 'Well this is all very awkward. I do wish you'd checked with me first.'

Prue shot him a look, 'Dad, you've been eating jam from the jar, and don't think we don't know about it because we do. You weren't about to agree to anything. Besides it's only for eighteen months. Then she'll be gone. Okay?'

Lord Ashcroft knew his children had his best interests at heart, and he did sometimes feel a little lonely. What he was most worried about was that he and Violet wouldn't get on, and that she'd discover his secret reading habit. Sighing he let his daughter take charge and was on his best behaviour with Violet.

❋ ❋ ❋

The first night Violet cooked her classic beef wellington, and it was really rather good. After a week of lasagne, chicken pie, pan-fried sea bass, chicken korma and steak and kidney pie, finishing with a roast on Sunday, Lord Ashcroft was well fed and felt like a king.

Violet was kind and pleasant. She liked the dogs, and Lord Ashcroft could sometimes hear her singing in the kitchen when she was preparing meals.

He'd forgotten what it was like to have a woman around and hearing her sing made him feel good.

After a month, Lord Ashcroft looked forward to Violet brining his toast and tea in in the morning, or sitting in the back garden with him for a mid-morning coffee.

'I can't call you Lord Ashcroft anymore.' Violet said with a wry smile one day. 'I've seen you in your pyjamas, I think we should be on first name terms.'

Lord Ashcroft smiled. Poor thing, she had seen him in his pyjamas, yes, she deserved to know. 'George.' He said glancing over his coffee cup at her.

'George? Why that's my most favourite name in the whole world.' Violet winked at him.

'Is it now?' Lord Ashcroft said.

'Do I get to call you Georgie when you're cross?'

'Not unless you expect me to call you Vi.'

Violet shrugged her shoulders. 'Fair enough.' she said. 'George it is then.'

They both sat quietly smiling while sipping their coffees.

* * *

The first Christmas was a great success. Violet cooked a huge goose, made some delicious mince pies and a traditional Christmas pudding complete with silver charms.

Prue was quite excited to see how things had developed between her dad and Violet, but was most disappointed when Violet received a silver thimble in her piece of Christmas pudding, and her dad had a silver button. However, both Richard and Hugo were delighted with Violet, particularly as she was great with the kids and offered to babysit while they grabbed a couple of date nights with their respective wives.

Prue sat in the kitchen with Violet and tried to probe. 'You are great with the kids. You must love families.'

'I do. I love children. That's why I want to leave for Australia. I have two boys out there; both are about to get married and I don't think grandchildren will be far behind. What I have I got here to stay for? I want to be with my family.' Violet said.

'So, you don't see yourself staying?' Prue enquired.

Violet turned from a boiling pan of potatoes to look at Prue. 'Don't get me wrong Prue. This is a nice job. Unexpected. But it is not going to be forever.'

Prue nodded sympathetically, perhaps she'd got it wrong. Prue asked, 'So when do your boys get married?'

'One is getting married this spring and the other this autumn, of course that's their autumn and spring because it's the other way around to here. I have flights booked. Don't worry. I'll freeze food for your dad, it'll only be a couple of weeks each time.'

Prue batted away the concern, saying, 'If the worst comes to the worst, then you might find he has been at the jam cupboard, but other than that he'll be okay.' Sipping their wine, Violet and Prue laughed.

* * *

In all honesty Lord Ashcroft did indeed raid the jam cupboard when Violet was away in the spring for her son's wedding, but not because she hadn't left him with plenty of delicious food in the freezer. It was because he missed her and was comfort eating sugar to avoid the way he was feeling. In fact, he was so happy to have her come home that he met her at the train station with her favourite flowers: freesias, and carried her bags. Violet was most flattered. George was just happy to hear her singing from the kitchen again. It felt like home.

By the time the second trip in autumn came around Lord Ashcroft was starting to feel a little down as he walked her to the train station, so she could catch her train to London and on to Heathrow Airport.

Violet tried to cheer him up. 'If I call your Georgie, will it make you smile?'

'No, it will not Vi, and you know it.'

They laughed.

Violet continued, 'I've made you lots of meals.'

'Yes, you have.' Lord Ashcroft confirmed.

'You know how to use the microwave?'

'Yes. Yes, I do.'

'It's only two weeks. I'm sure the time will fly by.' she said.

'It will for you.' said Lord Ashcroft in a sad voice.

'Do you want to come?' Violet asked.

'No, I'd feel like a sore thumb, besides I've got very important estate business to do. I can't possibly leave.'

Violet gave him a hard look. She knew he could come if he wanted to. Besides, Richard had come down to look after the estate before and was quickly learning the ropes. Violet knew he was worrying about something. Working it through. 'Okay then. Well. See you in two weeks.' Violet said.

Lord Ashcroft looked sadly into her eyes. 'Yes, see you in two weeks. Have a lovely time, won't you?'

* * *

The second trip was not very comfortable for Lord Ashcroft at all. It seemed more like a month than two weeks. He looked at himself in the mirror. He looked tired and old. He'd once been young and handsome. Really could anyone love this? He looked critically at himself and shook his head sadly as he walked away from the mirror. Besides, only another four months and she'd be gone forever anyway. He let out a deep sigh.

Lord Ashcroft was overjoyed when Violet returned. So much so that he forgot to cover his tracks and accidently left out the latest romance novel he'd been reading. He was absolutely mortified when Violet found it open in the library and poked her head around his study door, holding the book aloft and saying, 'I know I haven't read it, so this must be you.'

Lord Ashcroft looked up in horror. 'Absolutely not. I don't know what you're talking about.'

Violet came into the study and stood very still as she said, 'You know my dad died of Alzheimer's. One of the worst ways to go. I've watched the film a hundred times. We should watch it.' There were tears in her eyes. She was perfectly serious.

Lord Ashcroft rushed to get a tissue, and gently handing it to Violet said, 'It is a truly terrible disease. I'm sorry for you. I don't want to upset you. Do you really think you want to watch a film about it?'

Violet nodded through her tears. 'Yes, because it helps me to connect emotionally to the way I feel about the disease, and it's a beautiful love story. I don't want to spoil the ending of your book though.'

Lord Ashcroft said tenderly, 'Not at all. You won't spoil the book. If you get the film, then we can watch it together.'

* * *

A couple of days later Violet returned with a DVD from the post and placed it on Lord Ashcroft's study desk. 'Your place or mine?' she asked.

'Oh, definitely mine. I'll bring the bubbles too.' he

smiled.

'Done.' Violet said.

That evening Lord Ashcroft and Violet sat down to watch *The Notebook*. By the end Violet was sobbing, and so was Lord Ashcroft. After that, they quite often watched a romantic film late in the evening, and Lord Ashcroft felt relieved that he didn't have to keep his secret passion a secret anymore.

* * *

By the time the second Christmas came around, Lord George Ashcroft was completely in love. The scent of her, the way she tucked her dark-red hair behind her ears, her laugh, her gentle singing. The way she teased him, but not too much. He was in agony. He didn't want her to go. But what could he do? Perhaps he should propose? Would she stay? Would she say that he was too old and that it wasn't part of the agreement?

Lord Ashcroft twisted himself in knots about it, but when (to Prue's design) he received a silver wishbone in his Christmas pudding and Violet received a silver bell he took it as a sign. Sure of himself, he planned how he might propose to Violet.

The family left between Christmas and New Year. So, on New Year's Eve, Lord Ashcroft arranged for a movie night and bubbles, and while they were watching the movie, for there to be a surprise fireworks display in the estate grounds, so that Violet might be tempted outside, see the display and accept his proposal.

Everything went according to plan.

'What's that?' said Violet going to the window. 'Oh! It's a fireworks display, George, come look.'

'So it is.' Lord Ashcroft said. 'Let's put our coats on and go outside to look at it properly.'

Quickly putting on their coats they rushed out into the garden to watch the incredible display just over their heads.

'Violet?' Lord Ashcroft said.

Violet turned around to face him and he dropped to his knee. From his pocket he pulled out a beautiful emerald and diamond engagement ring. 'Violet, I have never felt love like I do with you. Please. Please don't go. Would you do me the honour of becoming my wife?'

Violet looked shocked, then she looked sad, then she shook her head. "No." She said in a small whisper. 'I'm so sorry George, I love you too. But we only have two out of three, and I want to be with my family.'

Lord Ashcroft stuttered in shock. He'd been so sure. He couldn't quite understand what she was telling him. 'T-t-two out of three? What do you mean? What is two out of three?'

Violet explained, it's the three C's George: chemistry, communication and compatibility.'

'But we have chemistry!' he exclaimed.

'Yes, we do.' Violet confirmed.

'And we have communication.' he said, exasperated.

'Yes. But we aren't compatible.' she said sadly.

'What do you mean?' Lord Ashcroft was confused.

'I mean, I want to go and you want to stay. We can't make it work. I'm sorry.' With tears streaming down her face Violet ran back indoors. Leaving Lord Ashcroft on his knee, holding a beautiful diamond and emerald ring.

* * *

Violet had a month left. And for the whole of January neither of them mentioned *that* night. But it hung in the air like an unopened present. The more they knew they couldn't have each other, that it couldn't work, the more they wanted each other.

Soon it was the season of lasts. The last steak and kidney pie, the last film night, the last bottle of bubbles.

Every fibre of Lord Ashcroft's being wanted to reach out and touch her, to plead with her to stay. But he'd given it his best shot and she'd said "No." What else could he do?

The last evening was torture. They both tried to be cheerful over dinner, but it was false. Violet looked close to tears most of the time, and to be honest so did Lord Ashcroft. So, he tried to keep his remarks to the weather and asking if she'd packed, several times.

The next morning, he drove her to the train station in his car. She was travelling to London today and would catch her flight tomorrow. She'd sent most of her luggage over already and was only travelling with one suitcase and one handbag. Her life was packed up from Cornwall. Soon she would be gone. Forever.

Lord Ashcroft waited on the train station platform with Violet and helped her with her bags onto the train. Then, with tears streaming down his face he stood outside the carriage window, as she slipped in to her seat. Raising his hand to the glass he whispered to her, 'I love you.'

Raising her hand to the glass to perfectly match his she mouthed back, 'I love you too.' Her eyes were full of tears.

The guard blew his whistle. Lord Ashcroft was asked to stand back from the train, and slowly, painfully, he was separated from his only love.

* * *

Lord Ashcroft was beside himself when he returned to Buxton Manor. He couldn't settle in his study and he was grumpy with his dogs. Even a spoon of jam from the jar and a bit of the quiche Violet had made and left for him didn't suit him at all.

That evening, he watched *The Notebook*, and with the music still haunting him, he quietly took himself off to bed.

* * *

'Excuse me, miss? The man said at Melbourne Airport. 'I'm looking for a Ms. Violet Penover?'

'Yes?' Violet said. 'That's me.'

'I have an important message for you.' The man handed her a bunch of flowers with a little, attached envelope.

Violet looked puzzled, took the flowers (a huge bouquet of freesias) and opened the envelope. Inside was written:

Will three out of three be okay? I'm arriving on the twenty thirty-five evening flight from Singapore. Marry me. George x.

Violet cupped her hand over her mouth and tears of joy sprung from her eyes as she kissed the little envelope and replied to the flowers, 'Yes, George. Three out of three will work. I will.'

Exiting the terminal gate and wheeling her suitcase towards her waiting sons, she hugged them tightly and said, 'I have a little surprise for you. I think I'm engaged.'

11. MISS NICOLA KLAUS'S ORPHANAGE FOR SPECIAL CHILDREN

Somewhere, in a remote part of Lapland, lived a kind-hearted young woman called Nicola Klaus. She had a small cottage on the edge of a dark forest, not far, but far enough for her own sanity and comfort, from a small village.

The summers were warm, the autumns were bountiful and the winters were cold. This winter was no exception. The snow was at least two feet deep already and drifting. Nicola looked out of the window. She wasn't concerned.

Nicola was a strong and confident young woman who knew her own mind. She was a little over five-foot-two; her build was stocky and strong; she had curly, mousey-brown hair, which was coarse to the touch; and the most sympathetic green-grey eyes you could hope to meet in a time of need.

Nicola's parents had taught her to be self-sufficient and she spent the summers and autumns carefully preparing for the winter snows. She welcomed the isolation. Nicola enjoyed her own company and she had her reasons for being alone.

Sitting in front of the fire, Nicola rocked gently in her rocking chair, stitching a new counterpane and quietly singing to herself. Her little brown dog was curled at her feet and her tabby cat sat at the window, looking out into the night; it was too cold to hunt unless it was in the barn. The mice were back and it was Huntmouski's job to keep the mice at bay and preserve the sacks of food through to the spring.

Nicola looked down at her little dog by her feet, saying, 'You warm there, Little Faithful? Time for a little trip outside before bed.'

Faithful tried desperately to ignore her mistress. It was cold outside! Besides, there was plenty of time for dozing before . . . *Woof*! Faithful jumped up. *Woof. Woof. Woof.* Faithful stood taught looking at the door. Her owner had to know. There was somebody out there.

Huntmouski glanced out of the window and jumping down arched her back at the door and hissed.

Nicola put down her stitching, carefully placing it on her wooden rocking chair. Going to the cupboard she pulled out her shotgun and loaded two cartridges. She'd had problems from troublesome villagers before. But she wasn't afraid. She was ready to defend her home if she had to.

Nicola went to the window and peered outside. The snow was falling softly in the light of the moon. There were footsteps leading up to and away from her front door. It looked like whoever had approached, had gone. Still. It was worth giving them a little reminder. Nicola opened the door and aiming her shot gun, she fired a shot into the air.

Nicola's little house was in a large clearing with a lake in the distance. She could see a good distance all around. Whoever it was that had come to her door must have run like the wind to get away.

The shot reverberated around the clearing and the sound got lost in the falling snow. To Nicola's shock, from not more than a few footsteps away came, '*Waa, waa, waa.*'

Nicola stood holding the still smoking shotgun and looked down in disbelief. For there on her doorstep, wrapped up tight against the cold, was a little baby in a fur lined basket.

Nicola rushed to put down the gun safely, and retrieve the baby from the cold. All she could think was, "My goodness, what were they thinking? If I hadn't found the baby, it could have died." Nicola retrieved the baby and fur basket. Deliberately locking the door, she went back to the fire and carefully removed the crying baby from its cosy nest of fur.

Nicola didn't know a lot about babies, but she guessed this little one to be about six months old. Cradling it to her shoulder, she cooed and shushed until the tiny thing quietened and fell asleep.

Quite frankly, Nicola couldn't believe it. What

mother could abandon her child? However, it wasn't long before Nicola discovered the reason why. When she removed the baby's little hat, she found that the baby had little pointed ears. It was a deformed child.

One of the unfortunate realities of a small community, and lots of cousins marrying cousins, was that now and again a genetic deformity would pop up. However, the villagers were suspicious and believed that these children were cursed. Quite often the children would "disappear" in the night or "go to stay with Granny" so as not to embarrass and bring shame on the family. Perhaps the mother believed that as Nicola was a loner, she would be prepared to bring up her child. It was quite an imposition, but thankfully Nicola had a kind heart and endless empathy.

Nicola named the baby Elsie. Throughout the long, cold winter Elsie and Nicola cuddled up together, and by the time the spring thaw came, it was as if they'd always been.

* * *

Nicola wasn't exactly cross. But she wasn't entirely happy with the situation. For the very next winter two more babies were left at Nicola's door. This time a little boy with webbed fingers and toes, and a little girl with six fingers. Nicola was going to need to think of a way to support them all. She was starting to feel a little busy. When the babies had gone to sleep each evening, Nicola spent her time furiously sewing and stitching; making counter-panes and cushions, aprons and tea cosies. Nicola was quick and neat with her needlework and had a good eye for colour. Her work soon became quite fashionable and it was as much as she could do to keep the village shop supplied. The village shop owner also sent her wares further afield to be sold (for a small commission). Somehow, by the luck of the gods, Nicola and the babies always had enough food and firewood to survive the winter.

The little babies grew to toddlers, and the tod-dlers to children. Every winter a couple more de-formed children arrived on her doorstep. Nicola hadn't the heart not to care for these poor un-wanted children, but this wasn't exactly how she'd planned her life. Nicola had to work hard and late every day and night to ensure the children were provided for.

A few more years passed and eventually Nicola found that she had fifteen children under her roof. Luckily, the older children were able to help with the younger ones, but she couldn't squeeze any more children into her attic bedroom (Nicola had long ago taken to sleeping in front of the fire). She wasn't sure how she was going to cope. The little cottage was bursting at the seams with laughing, happy, unwanted (now wanted) children.

Once again kind fate helped Nicola. A wealthy landowner from the south came to visit her in the spring. His wife was obsessed with Nicola's beautiful needlework. She had already bought three counterpanes and twelve pillows. The wealthy landowner was hoping that Nicola would take a commission to sew some more, as the couple lived in a large, eight-bedroom, wooden lodge, and there were plenty of beds still to cover.

When the gentleman saw how hard Nicola was working to feed and clothe the children, and keep them warm through the long cold winters, his heart wept with pity. He was well educated and didn't hold with the nonsense that children with deformities were "cursed". So, he offered to build an extension for Nicola, somewhere where the children could sleep at night and take lessons during the day, in exchange for sixteen counterpanes (one summer colourway set and one winter) and thirty-two matching cushions.

Nicola gratefully agreed and by the following autumn, a huge extension had been built on the back of her little cottage. The upstairs had over thirty beds (should more unwanted children happen to land on her doorstep) and the downstairs was filled with little tables and chairs, with a chalkboard at the front, so that the children could take lessons. The wealthy landowner had also hired a tutor for the children, as he believed very strongly in the virtues of a good education.

Nicola and the young tutor, Helga, got on very well, and between them they managed to navigate the following winter. Nicola taught Helga and the oldest children how to sew in her particular style, and when the children weren't learning they were creating beautiful counterpanes and cushions, kitchen linens and their new line of gifts (Helga's idea) of little rag dolls.

Nicola renamed her cottage: Miss Nicola Klaus's Orphanage for Special Children.

* * *

Elsie was nearly seven now, and the apple of Nicola's eye. Nicola sewed her a little bonnet that covered her pointy ears, but Elsie didn't feel self-conscious, because all the other children were just like her.

All the children were loved. Faithful and Huntmouski could have felt jealous if they'd had smaller hearts, but the wonderful thing with love is that there isn't a finite amount. The more you put out, the more you get back. So, the animals spent their days being petted and adored, played with and tickled. It was a perfect life and everyone had their place.

One evening, Nicola sat in front of the winter fire. Elsie cosied up to her lap and the other children cuddled around while Nicola read a story, and Helga prepared their warm milk for bed. As Nicola read, she felt that although she was tired and busy, she was so very happy and nothing could interrupt the quiet bliss they found themselves in.

After the story, the children had their milk and went to bed. Helga slept in the dormitory with the children, next to the babies' cots. Nicola stayed up a little later to finish the counterpane she was working on, when Faithful jumped from her feet and stood alert, pointing at the door. Woofing.

Anticipating it was a little delivery, but as always, being prepared, Nicola went to the window to look out. The snow outside their little orphanage was untouched and pristine. The clearing was quiet and the wind was calm. But the sky, oh, the sky was a riot of colour. Beautiful greens and blues, reds and oranges. The northern lights were spectacular tonight. It almost made the night seem magical.

Behind her, Faithful woofed again. Nicola drew her brows together and decided to investigate. She put on her long winter coat, furry boots, hat and gloves. She went to the cupboard and took out the shotgun, loaded it with two cartridges and put some spares in her coat pocket, then, opening the door, she peered outside.

Faithful was off like a bullet out of a gun. Faithful knew exactly where she had to lead her mistress. Nicola pulled the cottage door closed behind her and started to make her way across the pristine snow, under the fantastic light display in the sky above her. Something about the night felt special.

Nicola was much slower across the snow than Faithful, and it took her a good twenty minutes to reach the other side of the clearing, close to where one of the lanes passed by through the woods.

Woof. Woof. Woof. Instructed Faithful. Trying

desperately to make her mistress hurry.

'I'm coming, my sweet, I'm coming.' Nicola called.

Nicola reached the woods at the other side of the clearing and Faithful darted into the trees, towards the lane that passed through. Nicola followed her, to find that on the edge of the lane a sleigh had come off the road, and partially fallen into the ditch. The reindeers had managed to break their way free and were nuzzling for moss amongst the snow and the trees. Hurrying to the sleigh, Nicola found a man fallen in the snow, unconscious and very, very cold.

Nicola knew that she had to help him quickly, as hypothermia was likely already setting in. It would take too much time to go back to the cottage and get Helga's help. She'd have to do this herself. With a little luck and a huge amount of effort (Nicola surprised herself sometimes at how strong she was) she managed to haul the poor, cold man onto the back of one of the reindeers and she covered him in furs from the sleigh. Catching the reins in her hand, she jumped on top of the other reindeer and they made their way back across the clearing to Nicola's orphanage.

Nicola didn't want to wake Helga or the children. Somehow (she was sure it was hauling around sacks of grain that did it) Nicola found the strength to drag the man into her cottage on the back of one of his furs. Carefully, Nicola attended him and warmed him by the fire. His lips were blue. His face was wide and kind, with a brown curly beard and brown curly hair. He had a big nose and big bushy eyebrows. When Nicola removed his gloves, she found his hands were thick and calloused. He was clearly a hardworking man. Trying not to make assumptions, Nicola attended to him and stayed with him through the night, as he lay in front of the fire.

The next morning the children were agog at such a spectacle. They had seen other adults before, but their little sanctuary was predictable. It had been a long time since the wealthy landowner had visited, and they were not used to a man in the house. One of the babies started to cry. From his resting place near the hearth, the man stirred at the noise and started to wake.

As he opened his blue eyes, he stared around in fear at the little children peering over him. His brows came together in puzzlement. His eyes grew wide. When little Elsie leant forward to ask if he was okay, the man cried out and put his hands over his face shouting, 'Don't hurt me! Don't hurt me!'

Nicola was not impressed. Instructing Helga to take the children through for breakfast, she decided to deal with this herself.

Passing the man some warm milk, Nicola said, 'You crashed your sleigh last night. I pulled you out of the snow and brought you here. Your reindeers are outside and you are free to leave as soon as you feel better, but I won't have you scaring the children like that.'

The man protested; his blue eyes were wide with fear. 'But, but, they're deformed!'

Nicola was angry. 'Don't be so rude. I wish I'd left you in the snow now.'

The man looked quite taken aback and tried again, 'But they will curse your house and bring you misfortune.'

Nicola replied, 'Don't be so ridiculous. I've never heard such mumbo jumbo in the whole of my life.'

The man looked shocked.

From the kitchen dear little Elsie came in with a slice of warm bread and butter, and handed it to the man saying, 'I'm sorry I scared you, sir.'

In surprise, the man accepted the bread and managed to utter, 'Thank you.'

Nicola waited for Elsie to return to the kitchen, then crossly said, 'As soon as you feel well enough, please leave.'

A little under an hour later she found that the man and his reindeer had gone. And a little more than an hour after that he was back again, with his reindeer and sleigh, knocking on the cottage door.

Nicola opened the door, 'Yes?' she replied tersely.

The man shuffled in the snow on the doorstep and looked at his feet. 'Erm. I'm very grateful to you for saving me. And I see you have an orphanage. So, I, erm . . .'

'Yes?'

'Well, I'm a carpenter you see. I have a toy business. I have a sleigh full of toys, and as a thank you I'd like to give them to your orphanage. I do understand that without your help I'd be dead in the snow. And I'm sorry about scaring the little girl earlier. I didn't mean to. I'm sorry. I thought perhaps she'd like this little doll I made?' As a gesture of sincere contrition for being so rude, the man held out a little wooden doll.

Nicola was quite surprised. She hadn't expected to see him again. But she wasn't a proud woman and she knew that a sleigh full of toys would be most welcome. Calling to the children she allowed the man to unload his wares into her sitting room. It was almost as if Christmas had come early. The children were delighted. And they thought the man was quite possibly one of the best people ever. One by one they came up to hug him, say thank you, and gratefully accept their toys. After a while the man forgot to shudder at their deformities and looked a little overwhelmed at the happy, playing children.

Nicola also felt her heart melt a little and swallowing her pride, she said quietly to the man, 'Thank you. This really means a lot to them. I really am very grateful.'

The man looked happily into Nicola's lovely green-grey eyes and held out his hand saying, 'Nicolas. Pleased I could bring them a little joy.'

Nicola held out her hand, smiling and said, 'Nicola. I run the orphanage.'

* * *

After Nicolas left the orphanage, he found that he couldn't stop thinking about the children, Helga and Nicola. It really was quite extraordinary. His heart also warmed at the thought of the happy children, playing with the toys he'd made. Poor things, they weren't cursed at all. They were delightful children. Good-natured and sweet. He felt ashamed for his small-minded opinions and how rude he'd been.

Nicola and the orphanage had made such an impression, that Nicolas found that when he was passing again in the spring, he stopped by to see how they were all doing and bring them some more toys. The children flocked around him like a favourite uncle, Helga made a special meal, and even Nicola seemed pleased to see him.

Nicolas watched Nicola in awe as she ran the day-to-day business of the orphanage. She really was quite a woman. A force of nature. He felt sorry that she had the responsibility of all of this on her shoulders, and yet never once did he hear her grumble or complain. He could see that the children adored her.

After a few more visits, Nicolas adored her too. He'd watch Nicola hurrying around and working, fixing, mending or stitching. He nearly fell over in shock the day he saw her carry in a sack of grain in from the barn. Nicolas felt guilty that she was doing this all by herself, with no one to help.

Nicolas found that as the time passed, it was difficult to stay away. It became a regular thing for him to pop by as he was passing through, and when he wasn't there all his thoughts were of the orphanage, the children, Helga's wonderful cooking and Nicola: what an incredible woman!

* * *

One spring, when the flowers were blooming and the birds were singing, Nicolas cleaned his cart, brushed the reindeers, put on his best clothes, and travelled to Nicola's orphanage. He had a proposition.

Nicola, as always, was knee-deep in fabric and stitching, the children were outside playing and Helga was cooking lunch. Nicola took Nicolas into her little sitting room and settled back in her rocking chair, flanked by Faithful and Huntmouski, to continue to her work while Nicolas talked.

Nicolas cleared his throat. 'Nicola?'

'Yes,' she replied, rocking gently in her chair, her hands whizzing the needle over the counterpane.

'There is something important I need to ask you.' Nicolas continued.

Nicola stopped stitching and looked up at Nicolas.

Nicolas knelt beside Nicola and said, 'I really think you are quite an extraordinary woman; I am happiest when I'm here, with you and the children. I was hoping that you would let me marry you and join you here?'

Nicola sat very still for a moment before she replied, 'Nicolas, there is something I haven't told you.'

'Nothing you can say will make me change my mind. I am quite in love with you.' Nicolas insisted.

Nicola's mouth set in a grim line. Carefully, from under the counterpane she brought out her left hand, two of the fingers were fused together and her little finger was missing altogether. Slowly she said, 'There was a reason my parents moved out to this little cottage in the middle of nowhere. There is a reason I keep myself to myself. I have learnt over the years how to keep my hand hidden, so that no one will judge me. If you genuinely believe that deformities are a curse, then you need to know that I too am deformed.'

Gently, Nicolas reached forward and took Nicola's left hand in his own, raising it to his mouth, he kissed it and said, 'You are perfect to me. Nicola, I think you are an incredible woman. My proposition is this, let me join you. Let me come and make my toys. It gives me so much joy to see the children happy. I would like to join your orphanage to make toys for the children, but not just your children, all good, kind, loving children. What do you think?'

Nicola's heart melted all over again and leaning forward, she kissed Nicolas's lips as he knelt before her waiting for her answer.

Nicola drew back and said, 'I think that sounds like a lovely idea and I think we will be very happy.'

12. FINDING LOVE UNDER THE CHRISTMAS TREE

Keri knocked on her mum's front door. She was just trying to focus on holding it together. She could hear her mum's footsteps across the slate floor of the little cottage, then reaching the door she heard her as she fiddled with the key in the lock.

Keri turned around to look at the sleepy village in the morning light, watching the last cold wisps of night retreating behind hedges and parked cars. Frost stiffened the grass in the front garden and encapsulated the spider's webs on the rose bushes, which ran along the stone wall in front of her mum's cottage.

Pushing her glasses back up her nose, tucking a stray lock of black hair behind her ear, and hugging her checked coat tight around her, Keri heard her mum open the door.

'Oh, Mum!' Keri cried, and fell into her mum's arms, which were soft, warm and comforting.

Her mum was still in her dressing gown and her hair was a little dishevelled from sleep. She still had the warmth and smell of sleep, as she wrapped her arms tight around her daughter and said, 'Oh love. Come on in out of the cold.'

Keri left her hastily packed bags in the car. She dropped her handbag by the door, and her mum ushered her through to the living room, where they sat on the sofa next to the happily flashing Christmas tree. Safe in her mother's arms, Keri cried and cried.

* * *

After Keri had cried her heart out, and her mum had shushed and soothed her, her mum suggested a cup of tea. Keri nodded in agreement.

While her mum left for the kitchen to make tea, Keri got up and looked at her appearance in the mirror. Her black, pixie-cropped hair held neatly to her head, her heavy glasses and pleasant, open face looked just the same as always, but her grey eyes were puffy and red with crying. She'd cried a lot the last two days.

Keri knew they'd had problems, but she just didn't understand why it had come to a head at Christmas. She was also angry that once again he'd let his mum stomp all over them. It wasn't that her mother-in-law was the main problem, but she certainly didn't help, and Matt prioritising his mother's wants and wishes over her was the last straw. She just wished it didn't have to be this way. She did love him. But she couldn't take it anymore.

Keri looked sadly down at her hand to where her wedding ring had sat just yesterday. Is this who she was? The divorcee?

Keri's mum came back into the living room with two cups of tea, and Keri joined her on the sofa. As she sipped her tea, she could feel her hurt and upset bubbling up inside her again. Hot tears filled her eyes and spilled down her cheeks.

'Oh, Mum. Why did he do it? Why did he let her stomp all over us?' Keri said.

Her mum shook her head and set her mouth to a grim line. 'I don't know, love.' she said. 'It was when she went house hunting for you behind your back that I really started to understand how controlling she was.' Her mum shook her head again. It was comforting for Keri to know that she wasn't imagining it. That this wasn't right.

Matt had tried to gaslight her. To tell her it was in her head. But it wasn't right. He said that living between her and his mother was like a cancer growing between them. He said . . . What upset Keri the most was that she'd tried so hard. Because she loved him. Fresh hot tears welled up in her eyes and spilled over. 'Oh, Mum. I do still love him. How can I be here?'

'Shh.' Her mum rocked her baby girl in her arms. 'Shh. There, there.'

* * *

As it was Boxing Day, her mum wanted to go

to church. So, Keri was left alone in the cottage to start preparing lunch. It felt good to be active and not crying. It took her mind off things. Her brother, Paul, his wife and her niece would be over for lunch too. Keri was glad to see Paul, but she felt like such a failure. She was divorcing the man she loved because she was downright miserable and she just couldn't take the pain anymore. Was she insane?

No messages from Matt on her phone. No missed calls.

Keri tried to keep busy peeling potatoes and chopping carrots to go with the roast turkey. At least her family understood.

Her mum returned from church an hour before her brother and his family arrived, and she helped Keri with the last of the cooking. Keri's niece was delighted to see her, and her sister-in-law was understanding and kind. Keri tried to be honest about everything that had happened, tried not to cry and was just grateful that at least she had somewhere to go.

The family spent the afternoon playing board games and watching Christmas films on the TV. Paul, Keri's brother, came back in from outside after smoking a rollie. 'Hey, Sis,' he said to her, 'You fancy coming to the pub for a drink?'

Keri was about to say, "Yes" when both her sister-in-law and her mum chimed in saying they wanted to come too. Everyone looked at Keri's eight-year-old niece, watching cartoons and completely oblivious. Keri felt guilty, she couldn't exactly expect her mum to babysit when she'd just imposed herself on her at short notice, and she understood why her sister-in-law wanted to go. Keri broke the stalemate by offering to stay. Besides, she wasn't exactly looking pretty at the moment, with her puffy face and red eyes.

Snuggling up with her niece on the sofa and wrapping a fleecy blanket around them, Keri and her niece tucked into the Lindt chocolates while the "grown-ups" went to the pub.

Keri's family returned about an hour later. Merry from the sherry and bubbling with gossip. 'Did you have a nice time?' Keri asked from her cosy spot on the sofa.

Her mum replied, 'Oh it was great. Everyone in the village seems to have had a good Christmas. The bell ringers were out too. I think they're heading down to the church later.' Her mum hung up her coat. 'Oh, and Jackie from up the road has left her husband.' she blurted out. Trying to cover her insensitivity she gave Keri a quick kiss on the head, saying, 'See, so it's not just you that has the grotty husband.'

Keri smiled wanly. She still hadn't heard from Matt. But that was how he handled every conflict: stonewalling, withdrawing, silence. Because he was always the victim. But he was in pain (she reasoned) because by leaving she had caused him pain. Perhaps it was better to hurt herself than hurt him? Keri mustered her courage to her and replied, 'Thanks Mum, yeah, I'm sure I'm not the only one. No fun though.'

Her mum continued to gossip, 'Well, it's been on the cards for a while. Don't you remember that trouble over their son's primary school teacher. He definitely had an affair. She's well rid.'

Keri sighed. She was just another number in the cesspool of failed marriages and "I told you sos". This wasn't what she'd planned for her life.

Paul said, 'Oh, and Dan was at the pub. He was asking after you.'

Keri was surprised. 'Dan? How is he?'

Dan had had a crush on Keri pretty much all of their teenage years. Dan liked bikes and engines. He now worked in tractor repairs; he had his own business. He used to look at Keri like she was the sun. But he hadn't been good enough. Yes, he was extraordinarily good looking: tall, muscly, warm blue eyes, curly brown hair. But he'd never wanted to go anywhere or be anything. He'd been content to stay here and Keri had wanted more. He'd taken her on a date once, as a dare. Nothing had come of it. Keri hadn't really been that interested. She'd always been fond of Dan though. Coming back here and living a mundane life wasn't what she'd wanted, it wasn't what she'd planned. However, on reflection, what she'd been chasing hadn't exactly turned out to be her happy ever after, had it?

Paul replied, 'Yeah, all right. His business is doing well. Tractors always need fixing. When I said you were here, he talked about popping by.' There was an awkward silence. Paul had obviously said a bit more than that, but he didn't want to embarrass his sister. Plus, it wasn't as if this was the first time she'd left her husband.

Keri knew she wasn't happy, her friends and family knew she wasn't happy, and they were all concerned. Keri was lucky to have people in her life that cared about her. She said, 'Thanks Paul, yeah, that'd be great. I'd love to see him.'

Paul smiled. 'That's what I said.' Paul tweaked his daughter's ponytail. 'Right young lady, time to go home.'

Keri's niece protested, but it was of no use. In a flap of carrier bags and boxes of cold turkey to take home, Keri's brother and his family left.

Keri spent the rest of the evening sat on the sofa, in front of the fire, watching Christmas films and sharing a bottle red wine with her mum. Sometimes healing happens through the simple things.

✳ ✳ ✳

The next morning Keri had a slow start. She'd stopped crying at the drop of a hat, but she wasn't exactly energetic. So, it was no surprise that when Dan came around to visit mid-morning, that Keri was still in her heart patterned pyjamas and dressing gown.

Dan's familiar face popped around the living room door, saying, 'Hey Keri, you all right?' he asked in his cheerful way. Same warm blue eyes and curly brown hair. Same smile.

Keri looked up and gave an upside-down smile. 'Not really.' she sighed. 'But I've been here before. Right?'

'Aw, lass. Don't be so hard on yourself.' said Dan.

Keri's mum interjected, 'Tea for everyone?'

'Thanks Helen.' Dan replied. 'Love a cuppa.'

Keri's mum discretely popped the teas on the coffee table and busied herself in the kitchen, while Dan and Keri chatted by the flickering Christmas tree.

Dan listened quietly without judgment while Keri talked it out. In a few places he allowed himself a shake of the head, but that was about it. When Keri finished, he summed it up with, 'I understand you are trying to be fair, and look at it from all sides, but you don't sound very happy to me, and whichever way you slice it, that's the truth.'

Keri tried to keep the tears down, but Dan had pretty much nailed it. Keri tried to reply, 'I'm . . . I'm . . . I'm not happy.' and burst into tears.

'Aw, lass.' said Dan. With sad eyes he sat next to her on the sofa, put his arms around her and said, 'Hey, it's all right, home now, eh?'

Keri felt warm and safe being held by Dan. One of the hallmarks of her marriage was that she'd felt unprotected, vulnerable, unsafe, all the time. Is this how it's supposed to be? Are you supposed to feel safe in relationships? Or is it your fault if you don't?

Dan let her have her cry. When her tears subsided, he passed her her tea and suggested, 'Why don't you come with me, to the pub tonight, play some pool and forget about all of this?'

Keri nodded sadly. She just wanted to feel normal again.

* * *

Keri felt a bit nervous about going "out" to the pub. She hadn't really thought about nice clothes to go out in. So, she just wore her best jeans and boots with a chunky jumper and her checked coat. It was good enough.

Dan dropped by the cottage and walked up the road to the pub with her. The evening was cold but it was fine, and despite the village streetlights, they could still see the moon and the stars. Keri had forgotten how nice it was to be home. She felt safe here.

Their conversation soon turned to when they were kids, riding bikes and making dens, and when they got older making campfires and underage drinking. By the time they got to the pub, Keri was almost laughing.

Keri knew most of the people in the pub, and they certainly remembered her. For the first twenty minutes she was probed with questions: How was her job? Where was she living now? Was she back for long? Everyone avoided talking about Matt, which meant word had got around and they all knew. It didn't bother Keri too much, because she had a choice: she could stay unhappy or she could be the divorcee and free. Two days ago, she had chosen the latter. This was the start of a new life and a new path. She just had to be brave and walk it.

Dan was a gentleman and insisted on buying the drinks. He also secretly let her win the first two games of pool, and said she still had great aim with the cue (she didn't). The pub music list was entirely Christmas songs and there was a rainbow-coloured Christmas tree dancing merrily in the corner. Keri found herself unwinding, relaxing, and starting to feel *happy*.

Dan walked Keri home and suggested that to-morrow they go for a walk up on the moors. Perhaps it was the wine. Perhaps it was the Christmas spirit. Perhaps it was she was starting to feel less unhappy. But much to Keri's surprise, she said, 'Yes.'

❋ ❋ ❋

Dan picked Keri up at ten the next morning. He was in his work van and had thoughtfully picked up some snacks for them to eat on the drive. He was also keen to stop at a pub for lunch too. Keri just tried to let go and go with the flow.

The morning was bright and crisp. Not too cold. Keri hadn't brought any rain gear with her, or walking boots, but she'd borrowed her mum's wellies and her coat was warm enough. Driving up over the moors was spectacular. Keri had forgotten how beautiful it was. No wonder people wanted to live here and house prices were so high. Keri looked around Dan's van. How did he afford it? To live in this part of the world doing the job he was doing? Perhaps Dan hadn't got it wrong. He was doing a job he loved, in a beautiful part of the world, surrounded by family and friends. Perhaps it was Keri, chasing impossible dreams of other's ideals, that had missed the point entirely. What was she doing with her life?

The moors stretched out before them as far as the eye could see. They were up high and in places grey rocks broke through the scrubby green and brown grass. Twisted hawthorns and gorse bushes held themselves firm against the winter weather, waiting for the spring to flower gain. There were little streams to jump and small grey stone bridges, built centuries ago. It was as if this was a landscape to last all time. The air was fresh and the sky was endless. Keri drew in the pure air and exhaled all her hurt and sorrow.

It was lovely walking with Dan. It was so comfortable to be around him. He was easy company. Dan still looked at Keri with his warm blue eyes in the same way he'd always done. Like she was the sunshine. She didn't feel like anything special though. As they walked over the rocky, scrubby ground, he pointed out landmarks of interest and unusual plants or birds.

They walked to a high point and looking out at the vistas all around. Dan said, 'Do you remember when I took you on that date?'

Keri felt a bit awkward, but she owed Dan her honesty, he'd always been honest with her. 'Yes. I do.' she replied.

'I was completely in love with you back then.' he laughed at himself and threw a small stone into the air, watching it eventually hit the side of the hill and bounce down.

'I think I knew that.' Keri replied.

'But you weren't in love with me?' he asked.

'It wasn't what I wanted back then. I wanted to leave. To see the world.' Keri said.

'Is that what you want now?'

'No. I don't want to hurt anymore. I'd like to feel safe and happy.' Keri looked at her feet. 'I want to come home.'

Dan turned to Keri with tender eyes and she raised her teary ones to his, as he said, 'I don't want to you to ever feel unhappy.' Leaning down, he softly kissed her.

❉ ❉ ❉

Keri and Dan didn't talk about the kiss on the way home. Technically she was still married and she'd only left her husband a few days ago. Although, she defended herself, it wasn't the first time she'd left.

Dan pulled up his van in front of Keri's mum's

house. She could see the Christmas tree flashing through the living room window as dusk started to settle. Dan turned the engine off and they sat in silence for a few moments.

Finally, Dan spoke. 'I really enjoyed today, Keri. The walk on the moors. The pub lunch. I always feel good when I'm around you.'

Keri replied, 'I had a nice time too, Dan.'

Dan turned to her in the half-light and asked, 'Honestly, Keri, how do you feel when you're around me?'

Keri gulped, she was trying to be brave and name her feelings. 'Honestly? When I'm with you Dan I feel safe and I feel loved, like I'm standing in the sun.'

Dan smiled. 'That's about right then.' He took her hand and asked, 'Come have dinner with me to-morrow?'

Keri looked up to his imploring eyes. 'Yes.' she replied.

* * *

Keri had only brought one dress in her hasty packing, but she didn't want to wear it as she didn't want her mum to think one thing or another. Not that it probably made a difference, because her mum had already raised an eyebrow at her when she said she was having tea at Dan's house tonight. To her mum's credit she didn't say anything and just let her daughter be. Besides her mum didn't want to add fuel to the neighbour's gossip. Just a meal, nothing to see here.

Dan lived in a tiny, little cottage, squeezed in amongst other tiny, little cottages, in a terraced row at the top of the village, not far from the pub. Every room had steps up and down to it. Surprisingly the living room was able to take two small sofas and a TV with a stand. A small Christmas tree flashed rainbow-coloured fairy lights on the windowsill. It was amazing how Dan fitted it all in. Off from the living room there was a little galley kitchen with a small dining area the other side of the breakfast bar. There was also a downstairs bathroom with a showerhead over the bath. Some narrow, steep, enclosed stairs led upstairs to two bedrooms (one double) and a tiny study. It was almost like a little cottage hobbit house.

Dan was cooking curry. One of Keri's favourite meals. He'd remembered. Like the perfect host he was, he had "old school music" (from their youth) playing on the speakers and a bottle of red wine airing on the table. He insisted she sat down while he finished the cooking.

The meal was delicious. Dan had made everything from scratch. Keri couldn't help but be impressed, and completely forgave him that pudding was a shop bought ice cream. Dan took the wine bottle with them as they moved through to the living room. They talked and talked. Keri felt so comfortable. She felt as if she could be honest with him and tell him everything. It was a strange feeling to be listened to, taken seriously, not judged and to feel, safe. Keri hadn't felt safe in a long time.

Dan grabbed another bottle of red wine and they reminisced about the "old days" and funny things that had happened when they were growing up. How Keri's brother, Paul, had been chased by a bull. When Dan had found some keys left in a tractor and he'd decided to have a go at driving it. Keri couldn't help but laugh.

Dan smiled at her laughing and said, 'There she is! There's my Keri back again.'

Their eyes locked together, it was as if time had stopped and taken a breath. Leaning forward, Dan kissed Keri softly on the lips. She felt like she was falling into a soft, comfy bed. Keri felt warm and she felt loved. She felt safe.

Dan broke the kiss, took Keri's wine glass, and placed it on the windowsill next to his. He turned back to her and said, 'Surely you must know, Keri. I'm crazy about you. Always have been. Always will be.' and he kissed her again.

Keri pushed him back, 'But I'm technically still married.'

Dan shook his head, saying, 'Don't care. Got my Keri back again and that's all I care about.' Cradling Keri's face in his large soft hands, he kissed her again. He ran his hand around her neck and under the collar of her blouse. Keri knew where this could lead. She hadn't been properly kissed in years. Every part of her was buzzing with excitement. She made a choice, and closing her eyes she let their bodies take over.

* * *

Keri woke in Dan's bed with his body curled around her. She rubbed her head and grabbing her glasses and her phone from the bedside table, checked the time.

Dan kissed her shoulder. 'Morning Beautiful.' he said.

Keri put her phone down and turned to face him. Their eyes locked. He reached up his hand around her neck and said, 'You don't know how many years I've wanted to wake up next to you.' Her heart melted as she let his hands explore her body and he pulled himself over her.

* * *

It was late morning by the time Keri sheepishly arrived back at her mum's.

Her mum gave her a semi-stern look and asked, 'Nice dinner?'

'Err. Yes.' Keri replied.

'I know it's none of my business, but you're not divorced yet. Don't forget this is a village. People see, and people talk.'

Keri reverted to teenager as she said, 'Yeah. I know, Mum.'

'Just saying.' Her mum challenged back. 'Just

make sure you know what you're doing.'

Keri didn't really know what she was doing, but she knew how she was feeling. She was feeling warm, safe and loved. That had to be right. Didn't it?

Keri showered and spent the afternoon watching Christmas films. Dan had some tractors to fix today but he said he'd pick her up to take to the pub later to play pool. And then? Then she didn't know. Soon she would have to be back at work and making some life choices.

Just as dusk was starting to fall there was a knock at the cottage door. Keri's mum went through to answer it. 'Oh! Hello.' She heard her mum say in surprise. 'Come on through, she's in here.'

The living room door opened and in came, Matt. His six-foot frame filled the doorway. His "Ken style" hair was messy and askew. Matt's eyes were red with tears and he held a large bouquet of lilies. He sat down next to Keri on the sofa and said, 'I really love you. I do. I don't want a divorce. Please don't go.'

* * *

Keri's mum left Keri and Matt to talk in the living room while she was busy in the kitchen. Not her mess and she wasn't going to sort it.

In the living room, Keri's heart was in tatters. She'd married Matt because she'd loved him. But living with Matt was scary. It was like falling on a thousand swords every day. He was asking her to try again, to go to counselling. But he'd said that before and didn't go. He said he was sorry and wanted to make it right.

What should she do?

There was a knock at the door. Keri could hear Dan's voice in the kitchen greeting her mum and her mum saying, 'She's through here.'

Keri cringed as Dan came into the living room. She watched his happy, smiling face drop as he saw Matt with a large bunch of lilies sitting next to Keri on the sofa.

Matt looked at Dan and Dan looked at Matt. You could cut the tension with a knife. Instead, the Christmas tree stayed manically flashing in the corner and Keri said nothing.

Eventually, Dan said, 'Hello, Matt.'

Matt stood as he replied, 'Hello.' Matt turned to Keri, and said, 'Err. So, you're busy this evening I take it?'

Keri had to make her final choice now, and it would be forever. Both men stood looking at her.

Bravely, she stood up and said, 'Yeah. I am actually. Dan and I are going to the pub to play pool.' Then relenting a little she said, 'I'm sorry, Matt. I really am. I will always love you and I hope you understand. But we tried and it hasn't worked. I haven't heard from you for days now, because shutting me out is all that you do. I can't live like that anymore. I'm leaving because I want to be happy. I don't want to hurt you. But I choose me.'

Turning to Dan, she said, 'Pub?'

Dan tried very hard to hide the wide smile that was plastered across his face, as he replied, 'Yep.' And holding the door open for Keri, he followed her out.

Thank you for reading:

Snow Angels

and other short stories

I would be so grateful if you would give me a review. I have some other book suggestions below, and at the end of this book an extract from **Màiri**, a Scottish romance novel.

Happy Christmas! HL x

You may be excited to read from the Christmas Collection (on Amazon):

The Adventure of the Christmas Cracker
Three Christmas Presents

Also:

I Don't Do Affairs

I Won't Let You In
I Can't Marry You
Rich Man
Poor Man
Thief
Màiri
Isla
Dating Advice for Men

Coming in 2026:

Hiding a Thief
Catching a Thief
Loving a Thief
Meridah
The Secrets of Dating

and

Miss Scarlett Andrews Investigates
(Murder Mysteries)

HARRIET LOVEDAY

MÀIRI CHAPTER 1

Màiri turned her moss-green eyes to look out at the cool, grey-blue, autumn waters, which were swirling beside the golden sands of Cruden Bay. The salty air filled her nose, and above her, sea-gulls were buffeted and bounced by the breeze. On the horizon, far away, she could see a trawler ship slowly passing through the rough waves. Her eyes watched it lurch through the water until it was a tiny dot on the horizon.

Màiri swept a light-blond strand of hair back from her pale, heart-shaped face. She sighed. The sound was lost to the wind. Worry lines pinched her forehead and dragged down at her jowls. She let them stay.

She looked down at her faithful friend and companion, Fudge, as the wind played with his soft curls of snowy-white hair and his little legs shook with the cold. He had stuck loyally by her side for the last five years. In many ways, she was closer to Fudge, her West Highland terrier, than she was to her family. She loved these quiet walks with him; stolen moments of peace. He was a dear little thing.

Fudge sat obediently at Màiri's feet and watched her gaze as she looked out again at the cool, grey-blue waters. Her heart thought, "I wonder if he is out there now, on a trawler, bringing in the nets? . . I wonder if he died? But they'll never tell me, and I can't ask. I wonder what would have happened if. . ." her eyebrows pulled together sharply.

She shook her head and she gulped back at the tears that were stinging her eyes. Pulling in a last deep breath of the cooling autumn air, she turned her face from the sea.

Once again, the breeze played with strands of her hair that had fallen loose from her bun. It was as if the wind was taunting her and tugging at her emotions, as if it wanted her to cry.

Màiri made a low whistle for Fudge to follow her along the beach.

As if allowing herself one last guilty thought, Màiri let her eyes wander and look over at the sand dunes. A warm, deep glow, not forgotten, filled her body. It may have been more than twenty years ago, but here, in this little, lost, golden-sand bay, omitted by tourists and busy locals, was the place of her greatest happiness. They couldn't take that away from her because only two people knew. And it was likely only one of them was alive to remember.

Beating down her thumping heart, Màiri pulled in a deep breath, looked away from the dunes and gently released the memory to the breeze. She pulled her old, puffy, khaki coat tighter around her body, as dog and owner walked quietly along the beautiful, sweeping sands of Cruden Bay, in the cool, swirling, salty air of a quiet afternoon.

* * *

Fudge liked to sit right up front in the passenger seat and *woof* and *yap* at the passers-by.

As Màiri manoeuvred her old, grey, Volvo hatchback out from the parking space near the small harbour and headed towards the road, a sleek, black Ferrari with tinted windows smoothly pulled past her, along the road through the village.

Màiri clutched at her heart.

Suddenly, she worried she was going to have a panic attack – just like she used to. She shivered violently and took a deep breath. A cold chill flashed through her spine, her chest clenched painfully, and her breath caught in her throat.

Stopping the car sharply, Màiri caged her heart with rigid hands. Fudge stumbled on his passenger seat, and they watched the black Ferrari slowly slide along the main street and pull into the local council car park.

Màiri gasped for oxygen and sucked in her breath, refilling her body. Slowly, she regained her composure and the pain subsided.

She looked up from under her heavy eyes. Whose car was it? Cruden Bay was one of her favourite spots to walk Fudge; it was where her family had their holiday home. She hadn't seen a car like that around here before. Ever.

She shook her head, trying to let her troubled thoughts slide. Màiri put her car into gear and manoeuvred the large hatchback out of the small fishing village and north, up the road, past the council car park, past the sleek black car, towards the fishing port of Peterhead; the most significant fishing harbour in Scotland.

* * *

Màiri turned the steering wheel. She drove down into the wide bay, into Peterhead, through the houses, towards her family's beautiful, enormous Victorian villa. Her eyes wandered along the view of the bay before her.

She drove along the old streets with high pink-granite walls, guarded by high, twisted iron gates. Behind each wall lay a beautiful Victorian villa, built for the wealthy fishing families when Peter-head had been at the height of its fortunes.

Pulling through a pair of large, pink, Peterhead granite gate posts and onto a crunchy gravel drive, Màiri pulled past her parents' large house, which was made of thick granite walls, tall windows, high window gables, and carved, white-painted wood fascias. A house to last, a house to hold testament to its wealth. She steered the car slowly around the back, towards the garages. Tucking her battered Volvo neatly inside an open garage, she let Fudge out.

Fudge bounded into the enormous back garden, which was enclosed on all sides by the high granite walls. It was mainly left to lawn, with a few abandoned, leggy shrubs scattered about. Fudge sniffed and ran, hopped and bounced; a fluffy white dot in the rarely-cut grass. He was desperate to explore and sniff out any cats who might have dared to cross onto their land since he'd left just a few hours earlier.

Slowly, Màiri locked her car and crunched out onto the gravel. She looked up. Above her head, seagulls screamed and cried. She could smell the fish from the harbour even this far into town. Turning towards the house, her eyebrows rose. Her father's Porsche was parked messily around the side of the garages. Her eyebrows pulled together and her mouth tightened. He always parked in the garage and was never home this early. Her father was as predictable as a clock.

Ian Esson loved to work because he loved the money, power and control it gave him, and it was rare for him to be back before dinner most evenings. Màiri had once wondered if he kept another woman, but he was too busy for that. His business, "Esson Fisheries", was the largest private fishing company in the port of Peterhead. He owned eight trawler ships and nineteen smaller fishing boats, alongside several large warehouses and two fish shops; one here in Peterhead and one in Aberdeen, where her sister Lynne and brother-in-law Steve lived and worked. Ian was always busy, but even more so now that some of the trawlers and nets were getting repaired, ready for the start of the autumn fishing season for Haddock. There was work to do and Ian was the man to do it.

Màiri whistled to Fudge to come inside. She made her way past the enormous Victorian conservatory, which was flaking white paint like dandruff. Opening the old, thick, cracked-black-gloss-painted oak back door, Màiri held it for Fudge as he bounded in before her. She softly commanded him to wait, took off her leather ankle boots and reached up for his towel from the dark, carved-wood, Victorian coat rack, and started gently drying his little paws.

Fudge sniffed up at Màiri's face in familiarity; it was almost as if he was giving her a little reassuring kiss on her nose. Telling her that everything was going to be okay.

Looking into his large, dark, bulging eyes, Màiri affectionately tickled his head and tugged his little ears, saying in her soft Scottish accent, 'Darling little one. Mummy loves you very much. You're a good boy.'

Fudge made a small *woof* and bounded off, deeper into the house.

Màiri slowly took off her thick, padded coat and hung it on the rack. Inside the house, possibly from the drawing room at the front, she heard raised voices, and her father shout in his deep, thick, Peterhead accent:

'It's a monstrosity! He must have paid a backhander to the council to get *that* approved. A disgusting display of wealth, flashing his cash around. It's common. I cannae believe that the planning has got this far. I will talk to Robbie MacBride myself this evening. I won't have that jumped-up little *loon* throwing his money around here. I've put him in his place once and I'll do it again!' His 'rs' rolled heavily like the sound of thunder.

Màiri gave an involuntary shiver; she could hear the menace in her father's voice and she knew the consequences of it. She could just about make out the soft, sweet, soothing Scottish tones of her mother's voice, too quiet to hear the actual words, but the intention was clear; she was trying to pacify her angry husband.

In contrast, Màiri could also hear her mother's sister, Màiri's Aunt Anne, in her strong Scottish accent echoing back Màiri's father's indignation to him: 'I completely agree! Such a vulgar display of wealth is disgusting. And we all know it's *not* through hard work. Well, Ian, you know what they say, easy come, easy go. We will have the last laugh as we watch him fall flat on his face. Again. We'll watch him go.'

Once again, Màiri could hear the soft, sweet tones of her mother trying to calm the agitated adults, but her voice was overpowered by her husband replying, 'Aye, you're right there, Anne. And when the day comes, which will not be so far away, I will celebrate his demise with a dram of my thirty-year-old special Lochnagar single malt. Nothing will give me greater pleasure than to open *that* bottle to toast to his failure. It is a sweet irony. I'll be drinking something that is his complete opposite in every way; classy and refined!'

Fudge dashed into the drawing room, and Màiri could hear her mother loudly exclaim, 'Oh, little Fudge! You're all sandy and damp! Where is Màiri?'

Màiri wasn't sure, but she thought she heard her aunt say, "*Shh.*"

Uncertainly, Màiri walked through the grand hallway and gingerly poked her head around the drawing room door. Hesitantly, she slowly walked into the enormous room.

The room would have been the height of fashion and taste, thirty years ago. It had a garish red-and-brown patterned, thick wool carpet, which was decidedly thin along the threshold into the drawing room and around the massive, carved, pink-granite fireplace, which was a true testament to the craft of the Victorians. The open fire had been replaced years ago by a smaller, practical stove and tiled in with beige, iridescent, square tiles; in complete contrast to the heavy, dark-wood, Victorian furniture; and thick, red, velvet curtains. The room was about four metres square, and the tall, wide, bay window at the front looked out onto a relatively modest front garden.

The garden was separated from the streets of Peterhead by high, pink-granite walls that ran around from the front to the back and safely enclosed the property from less desirables. However, the large, black-gloss-painted but rusting in places, twisted iron gates lay open, and grass ensnared their base. It was as if someone had forgotten to close them long ago and then couldn't be bothered anymore. The opening led out to the road that ran through to the centre of town. The gates were never used (who would dare to cross *this* threshold uninvited?) and the pink Peterhead granite gravel tried to escape from the driveway onto the road, ready to be swept away by the industrious road sweepers.

The relatively modest area of lawn was parted from the main house by the large sweeping gravel drive as it crashed around the side of the house and swept through to the back, like the surge of the tide. A few large, leggy, unruly shrubs persisted in the front garden, not dissimilar to those at the back of the house, and they were clutching at the last of their leaves before the cold winter. There *were* a handful of impressively tall pine trees next to the front garden wall (where they would be seen) forever brooding, standing proud and looking down their noses at the passers-by outside the villa walls, but truth be told, they too should have been trimmed back years ago. Instead, they grew tall and mighty, too close to the enclosing high granite wall, which was starting to crack as they towered over it. Unaware, the dark-green pine trees loomed over the walls and gave snide hints to the passers-by of the mighty grandness of the property within, but failed to look behind, to see what it had become.

Inside the drawing room, in the centre of the room, hanging from the ceiling, was a beautiful cut-glass chandelier, held by a moulded ceiling rose with scrolls, grapes and delicate flowers. The cornicing around the room also had the same ornate moulding and was a reminder of the opulent wealth from another era, but the walls were magnolia with spots of damp, and the velvet furniture was threadbare in places; a dim memory of when they were new, and fashionable.

Màiri looked at the adults around her. Her father, Ian Esson, was pacing the room with his fists clenched. He was a huge man, standing at least six-foot-three and weighing possibly as much as sixteen stone. Màiri would never dare ask. His arms were thick and muscly, and his chest hearty and broad. Although he was over sixty now, he dyed his hair black, his skin was healthy and tanned, and his teeth glowed white. He liked to wear fine-cut suits and shirts over his thick, muscly torso. Today he wore some expensive designer jeans; a light-blue handmade shirt, open at the neck; and a thin, light-grey wool blazer. He wore a tan leather belt and tan Italian leather shoes. He was pacing through the room as he raked his hand through his hair, before clenching his fists again.

Ian looked over quickly as Màiri cautiously came further into the drawing room, and the irritation left his face as a neutral expression appeared. In his thick Peterhead accent, he said, 'I see you've come back from yer walk?'

Màiri nodded in deference, then looked over at her mother, who was sat on the end of an old velvet sofa near the stove. She was fussing with Fudge and looked similar to Màiri in almost every way, only twenty years older. Her face was lined and her features were delicate. She had the same fine, light-blonde hair, which fluffed and curled around her head and was kept artificially blonde by regular trips to the hairdresser. Just like Màiri, she had the same moss-green eyes and the same gentle nature; Margaret Esson was sweetly beautiful. She looked up from her soft seat on the sofa and asked Màiri, 'Did you have a nice walk, darling? Did you go to Cruden Bay?'

Màiri nodded, gulped, and said, 'Yes, I was hoping to see some seals but I couldn't see any today. The weather is fresh and fine though.'

Across the room, Màiri's Aunt Anne scoffed as she leant forward from her position on the other large sofa; her pinched nose and tightly held salt-and-pepper hair straining as she replied, 'Well, I'm glad at least one of us is calm and relaxed. I'll doubt you'll be so soon though, girl, when you hear the news. Nothing more than a testament to how low the council has stooped to take bribes. I'm quite sure they are desperate for money to line their pockets since your father has stopped being quite so generous.' And she shot Ian a significant look with her small, dark eyes.

Màiri raised her eyebrows at her aunt and turned to look at her father, whom she found had been watching her cautiously, as she asked, 'What is the news, Father?'

Ian Esson swallowed heavily and wrinkled his thick nose as he spat out, 'The council have approved a development. An enormous house! Some ridiculous glass and concrete monstrosity is going to be built to the south of the bay. On the site of one of our first warehouses, which you may remember we sold for development two years ago. Apparently, the whole area is to be "positively impacted" by this new building. And apparently, the house build is going to cost one million to build. At least! It's a disgusting waste of money.'

Her father started pacing again, and Màiri turned to look between her father and her aunt as she enquired, 'Who is it? Who's building this house?'

Màiri's aunt sharply replied, 'We have no idea, Màiri! But that's not the point. Clearly, there's been some backhanders at the council. No decent authority would allow planning for such a monstrosity. And on our land too!'

Màiri turned back to look at her father and found he was scowling at the floor, his clenched fists blanching of blood in his tight grip.

Trying to defuse the situation, Màiri said, 'I guess I'd better give Fudge a rubdown with a damp towel and try and brush the sand out of his hair.'

Màiri's aunt quickly added, 'I ask you to do that every time, girl. But you always forget. Sometimes I think you do it on purpose. I know we have a cleaner, but we do have to pay her. Something you seem to take for granted.'

Màiri gulped heavily and replied, 'Yes, Aunt, I'm sorry. He slipped out of my hands before I had a chance to wipe him down properly.'

She looked over at her mother, who was tickling little Fudge's ears and completely oblivious to her aunt's reprimands. All she could think about was removing herself from this angry, buzzy room and getting back to her quiet spot in the conservatory as soon as possible, so she could bury her head in a romance book and imagine herself away in her mind.